STAMPEDE!

The moon lit up the desolate scene. The cattle had passed west of the house destroying everything in their path, knocking down the barn, flattening the fences, running off the livestock. Only the house stood as mute testimony that the family had lived and worked here.

Pa walked toward Ma and Melody carrying a broken Mark. Pa was covered with dust and tears washed down his cheeks. "I just couldn't get to him. I was pinned against the house where I couldn't see or hear anything except those damned cows—hundreds of them trampling everything—an' behind them a dozen riders pushin' them through our place as if it weren't even here."

He carried Mark into the house placing him on the bed. Ma started washing his still body. Suddenly, without warning, the woman flung herself over his body and started to scream, "No! Not my boy! Not my boy!"

THE NESTER'S REVENGE

B. J. Whapeles

TOWER BOOKS   **NEW YORK CITY**

A TOWER BOOK

Published by

Tower Publications, Inc.
Two Park Avenue
New York, N.Y.   10016

One

Melody Grant surveyed the drab classroom with distaste and asked herself again what in the world she was doing here. Never, even in her most depressing nightmares, had she seen herself as a schoolmarm. That was a job for dowdy old maids; she was only nineteen and hardly dowdy. Besides, she had a man waiting to marry her just as soon as she was done with all this nasty business and was ready to go back to St. Louis, to be with him. If it wasn't for that rotten Winslow, she would be with him right now—dressed in fancy silks and sipping tea like a lady—instead of riding herd over boys much bigger than she was.

The noise from the other side of town was making it hard for any of them to concentrate on their studies. She knew the older boys wanted to be off to see what the commotion was all about. Although she had an idea it was caused, in one way or another, by the cowhands from the Winslow spread, she had no desire to see what it was about. She had seen enough of their kind of fun in her short life to last her an eternity. Anyway, she could get the details from Sam when she stopped by the newspaper

5

office on her way back to her room. Sam Farris was probably the only person in the valley who wasn't cowed in one way or another by H. J. Winslow. Unless you counted her—which Winslow didn't. But he will, she swore to herself, he certainly will.

She didn't realize that, in her anger, she had spoken the last words aloud until one of the boys said, "What did you say, Miss Grant?"

"Never mind, Charlie, just keep your mind on your work."

Her mind, however, was on the commotion at the other end of town. At that moment the afternoon stage was arriving with a great deal more fanfare than usual. It had been met clear out by the Miller place by a raucous gang of cowhands and escorted into town with whoops and hollers and blazing guns. The noise had kept the horses running at a full gallop well past the stage office.

A tall, lanky young man in his early twenties jumped down from the stage, waving his Stetson and whooping at the riders gathered around him. He wore range clothes much like the others' except his were mostly new; his boots and hat, although not new, didn't bear the marks of hard work. Chad Winslow greeted the few men he knew by name and turned to his father's foreman, who was standing close by. Socking him on the arm, Chad said, "Marty, you old bull, was that welcome necessary?"

Marty returned the familiar gesture. "Don't tell me you've gone city dude on us while you were at college. You know cowhands love any excuse t' make a little racket. After all, you've been gone a long time." He gestured toward the saloon down the street and said, "Now that yore growed, how 'bout joinin' me fer a drink 'fore we head back t' the ranch? Yore ol' man gave most of the boys the afternoon off."

"Speaking of the old man, where is he? I expected to see him here waving a large sign reading 'Welcome home,' or maybe one saying 'It's about time.'"

"He ran int' a little problem. You remember Shorty Johnson? He's worked fer us off an' on fer a few years. Well, he got int' some trouble with the law over at Silver City, an' yore ol' man rode over there this mornin' t' see if he could straighten it out. He should be back tomorrow. This here's gettin' t' be the only place a man can have a good time without the law gettin' in it." As he talked, the two men had been walking toward Sally's Saloon and dance hall where the other men had already gathered.

As he entered the saloon, Chad was greeted on all sides by out-thrust hands and slaps on the back. Most of the men around the crowded bar worked for the Winslow outfit. Working their way through the men, Marty and Chad found an empty table near the rear wall where they were soon joined by Sally carrying two beers.

Setting the beers in front of the men, she said, "I kinda figured ya would want these."

The owner of a full matronly figure, Sally wore a lavish amount of makeup—especially for so early in the day. But it didn't hide the fact that she was too old for the bright red hair that fell over her shoulders. Chad thought how lucky she was that his father had helped her open this place, since she was beyond the age for making much money hustling drinks or working the back rooms. With women becoming more plentiful, the men were getting harder to please.

She sat down next to Chad, filling his nostrils with the pungent odor of cheap perfume and whiskey. He remembered that he had never liked her much as she patted his knee playfully. "Well, Chad, how's it feel t' come in the front door an' sit with the big boys? I can remember when H. J. would bring ya int' the office in back an' give ya a little taste of beer."

"I've been gone quite a while. I've been in bars before in the East. I must say that your place is as nice as any I've seen." He meant it, too. His father had insisted that everything be top drawer; most of the fixtures had come from Chicago. When it was built, it had the longest bar in the territory, with a backdrop of ornate mirrors running the length of the wall. There was a small stage, which was only used on special occasions, and a large, polished wood dance floor. In the evenings, there were always a couple of faro games going and one or two poker games. The chairs around the card tables were leather and more comfortable than most. It was just dim enough, all the time, to make the girls all appear better looking than they really were. One thing that didn't add much class to the place was the piano, since the piano player rarely played anything well enough for it to be recognized.

Sally looked pleased. "Thanks, kid. By the way, where is yore ol' man?"

"Marty was just telling me when we were interrupted by well-wishers," he answered. Turning to Marty, he asked, "Can you tell me about it here?"

"You mean in front of Sally? Bet she knows as much about it as I do. You know that it used t' be well knowed all over the territory that no one—not even the law—messed with one of Winslow's crew. Things are changin' though. With the railroad comin' closer, more an' more non-cattle people are movin' in; merchants an' nesters an' married women—the kind what wants everything neat an' orderly fer their kids. Jest about every town but this one has a full time law man, who's stickin' his nose in everything."

"That looks like the wave of the future, and we had all better get used to it. I think that the new people may just add to the quality of life around here—if we give them a chance."

"I don't know 'bout that. All I know is Shorty got int' a fight in the saloon at Silver City, an' someone got shot. Now the townspeople are talkin' 'bout hangin' him. In the ol' days, no one would've dared even arrest one of Winslow's men."

"As I remember him, Shorty was rather a no-account, anyway. I can't believe this is the first time he has been in trouble with the law. Why is Dad so concerned about him?" Chad said with a puzzled look on his face.

"It ain't Shorty so much as the idea that someone would arrest one of his men. The Winslow name has always carried a lot of weight in this territory."

Chad finished his beer and stood up. "Well, I can understand that, but I don't think some troublemaker should use our name to cover up for lawlessness. Let's get going. I'm anxious to see the place again."

Marty studied the young man as Chad turned and started to make his way though the crowd. He had changed, that was for sure; not just by adding a couple of inches to his height either. Marty had the uneasy feeling that Chad's years in the East had softened him—took some of the cowman out of him. Having him back might not help H. J. as much as Marty had hoped.

"Are you coming?" Chad called back over his shoulder.

Marty followed him outside and took him around to the back of the building where a strawberry roan was tied. A slow grin spread across Chad's handsome face as he went to the horse and began patting him.

"I'll be dogged. It's Beau. How are you, old boy?"

Marty smiled to himself at the sound of that phrase mixed with Chad's educated talk. He was pleased that Chad remembered the horse, which H. J. had given to him when it was still a colt. Marty had let Chad help break it. It had been a good year for both of them.

"Figured ya might want t' ride back t' the ranch. I've told the cook t' take yore things in the buckboard."

Chad smiled with pleasure as he swung easily into the saddle.

Two

By the time Chad Winslow was on his way to his ranch, Melody had dismissed her students, cleaned the school-room, closed the door and was making her way gingerly through the muddy main street of Marysville. The small log schoolhouse had been hastily erected by the new school board when she had told Sam Farris that she would teach for a term or two. They had located it a half mile south of town, and about a quarter mile west of the main road in order to keep it away from the stage route and the cowhands' section of town.

The town consisted mainly of one main street and three side streets running off at right angles. These were rarely used, except by the people who lived in the few houses that had been plunked down here and there, because Main, which ran north and south, was the major road into and out of the town. Although there was no actual line, the northern and southern ends of Main were like two different towns. The southern end, where Melody now walked, was the newest part of town and had been built by the family men, who wanted a town their wives would be comfortable in. Besides the school and a partly built church, there was a general store, a new dressmaking shop, the livery stable where Melody boarded her horse, and Sam's newspaper office.

Bridging the two ends of town was the hotel. It was older than the other buildings, having been built for the cattlemen before the newer people arrived. The biggest and best kept building in the north end of town was Sally's. The rest of the town looked like a shabby replica of the cowtowns that had bloomed in the days of the long cattle drives: a gambling house, pool hall, brothel, and another saloon. Next to the stage office stood the blacksmith shop, and a barber shop was sandwiched between the pool hall and the hotel. Although not Dodge City, the town served the needs of the local cowmen very well.

Melody was glad that she could walk to school and back home again without going through that part of town. The town was changing for the better, but not fast enough for some, like Melody and the Farrises. Turning in at the newspaper, she could hear the noise from Sally's. It was a little early for things to be getting so loud, and she wondered briefly what the occasion was.

Sam looked up from his desk when he heard the door open. "Afternoon, Miss Grant. How were the children today?"

"As bored and boring as always. The little ones, like your two, are sweet, but trying to teach a half-grown boy is a very frustrating job, I can tell you. I sure couldn't take it year after year like some teachers do," she replied wearily as she lowered herself gracefully into the chair in front of Sam's desk. "Now, tell me what is going on down the street? All that noise made it harder than usual to keep the children's minds on their studies."

The middle-aged man leaned back in his chair, put his

hands behind his head, and rested his feet on his desk. He was thin to the point of skinniness and so fair that he almost looked ill. Actually, he was a healthy, energetic man, but in this country, where most of the men were leathered and bronzed by constant exposure to the sun and wind, he looked sickly by contrast. His voice was even a little thin as he answered, "Didn't I tell you that Chad Winslow was coming home today? All the ruckus was the Winslow crew welcoming him back. Any excuse for shooting, drinking, and fighting. He has been gone for over an hour, but most of the cowhands are still at it."

A frown crossed the girl's delicate face. "That whole bunch is impossible. What a stupid excuse to make a lot of noise. Why, in St. Louis, they would be put in jail for such behavior." Suddenly, she realized that she had been so irate about the noise that she had missed what Sam had said about someone named Chad. "Who is this Chad Winslow?"

"Chad Winslow is the only son and heir of H. J. Winslow. He has been back East attending college for the last few years. From what I've learned, he's not a bad sort. I was just writing a news item about his arrival back in our quiet little town." He turned his attention back to his work, and said absently, "Tell Lenore that I will probably be a little late for supper, will you? I have a feeling there will be something happening before these men all get through the night, and I wouldn't want ol' H. J. to miss reading about his 'boys' in the paper."

Melody laughed a little uneasily as she headed out of the door, well aware of how Sam's news articles about his cowhands affected Winslow. Sam had had too many threats about them not to know H. J.'s stand on the paper.

When she reached the Farrises' house, where she was staying, she found Lenore Farris in the kitchen building up the fire in her cook stove. Two of the children from Melody's class sat at the large kitchen table with their reading book opened between them. A smaller child weaved his way around the chair legs, and Lenore balanced another on her hip. As Lenore smiled at her, Melody was again struck by the surprising beauty of that smile. One day, before all the hard work and children, she bet that Lenore had been a real beauty. Now, too plump, she wore a permanent crease across her forehead from worrying about Sam—a crease which deepened when Melody gave her Sam's message.

"Oh, Melody, why does he have to badger Mr. Winslow so? He could find plenty of news around here without angering that bunch." She shifted the baby from one side to the other, and asked, "Did you read what he wrote about that Shorty Johnson business? It's bound to get him in trouble."

Melody nodded affirmatively. "Lenore, you know that he wants to see this town grow and be a fit place for you and your children to live in. And don't forget about all the people who have been hurt by Winslow's lust for power and money." The anger of her words startled even herself.

The older woman smiled reassuringly at her. "I know Melody, and I'm proud of him. It's just that I worry so about him. Heaven knows what I would do with four kids all by myself around here."

"I know." Melody started for the stairs. "If supper is going to be late, do you mind if I take a ride? It has been awhile since I've been out on Fortune."

After changing into her riding costume—a pair of

men's denim pants, shirt, boots, and Stetson—Melody walked to the livery stable to get Fortune. Even in St. Louis she had hated to ride sidesaddle in all those cumbersome petticoats and long dress that her Uncle had preferred her to wear. Here, she had an even better reason for the get-up.

With summer approaching, it was staying light longer, and she was hoping to take advantage of the added daylight to become better acquainted with the surrounding country—especially the Winslow holdings. Fortune heard her coming and started whinnying and dancing around in his stall. The horse had taken an instant liking to her when she had bought him a couple of months before, and he obviously liked to be ridden, especially out in the country, which suited her fine since she loved to ride. Having saddled the horse, she gracefully swung up on his back and soon was riding away from the last buildings at the edge of town.

Away from the noise of the town, she drank in the quiet and the beauty of the surrounding country. She had been surprised at how much she loved the jagged Rocky Mountains surrounding this valley, turning an ever-changing face toward the sky. In all those years in St. Louis, she had forgotten how much she had once loved the native grasses, the mixture of evergreens and cottonwoods that covered the mountain slopes, and the singing streams which made their way to the lazy Basin River which rolled on through different, ever bigger rivers until it finally arrived in the mighty Mississippi which had flowed past her house in St. Louis. Now, she remembered her childhood delight in this land and felt a great need to see the Chaffin place. She hadn't been back there yet. She had been afraid of the memories it would stir in her. Now, she felt she was ready.

Finding a semblance of a road that she thought would lead her to her destination, she followed it until she ran into a barbed wire fence. It was Winslow's fence; the irony of it being here on the old Chaffin place galled her. Next time she came out here, she would bring something to cut it with, but this time she decided to see if Fortune could jump it. The horse had shown a remarkable flare for jumping from the first, but this time he outdid himself by easily topping Winslow's fence. A few yards beyond she could see the neglected log cabin that had once been a house. Home, she thought, as her mind drifted back to the last time she had seen the place.

She had been eleven that summer, and life had been good. It was the second summer they had been on their claim, and her father had finally finished their house. After Mark plowed the land, she and Ma had planted and cared for the large vegetable garden in anticipation of having something besides venison and homemade breads as they had the last winter. Even her Ma had stopped saying they were fools to come out to this god-forsaken wilderness, and seemed to be enjoying her new home. Her only complaint was that there was no church or school around. Of course, they read the Bible every-day, and Ma taught the two kids how to read and do sums, but Ma said it wasn't the same as going to school and church.

She had been Melody Chaffin then; she, her brother Mark, and Ma and Pa had been happy until Winslow got tired of waiting for them to starve out and leave what he still considered open rangeland. All the hard work and happiness had been wiped out one brilliant fall night.

She had just climbed the ladder to her loft bedroom

when she heard a low rumbling sound off in the distance. In a short time, the sound swelled into a heart-stopping roar. Later, she couldn't remember having climbed down the ladder, but there she was in the main room clinging to Ma as Pa headed out the door. Mark was outside finishing some after-supper chores, and her parents were worried about him. By this time, the bellowing noises and the shouting men had signaled them all that they were right in the path of a herd of stampeding cattle.

"God help us," Ma cried as the noise and dust grew worse. She held Melody close enough for the girl to bury her face in Ma's apron to keep some of the dust out of her nose and eyes. It seemed an eternity before they were sure that the cattle were all gone, and they carefully opened the door and stepped outside.

The moon lit up a desolate scene little resembling the landscape of yesterday. The cattle had passed to the west of the house destroying everything in their path; knocking down the barn, flattening their fences, running off their few head of livestock, and leveling their cherished garden. Only the house still stood as mute testimony that they had lived and worked here.

A low moan from her mother turned her attention toward Pa who walked toward them carrying a broken Mark. Pa was covered with dust and tears washed a streaked path down his cheeks as he said, "I just couldn't get t' him. I was pinned against the house where I couldn't see or hear anything except those damned cows— hundreds an' hundreds of them trampling everything— an' behind them a dozen riders pushin' them through our place as if it weren't even here."

He carried Mark into the house placing him on their bed in the corner, and from the pail of water that Mark had brought in earlier, Ma started gently washing his still body. At first, Melody didn't realize that he was dead, because her mother was so quiet and methodical as she worked over him. Suddenly, without warning, Ma flung herself over his body and started to scream, "No! Not my boy! Not my boy! Oh, my God, no!"

Pa, who had been standing quietly by the bed, put his arms around her trying to comfort her. He was crying, too, when he said, "Must have been Winslow's cowhands. There ain't any other cattle outfit in Basin River Valley, an' no one else drives his cattle through this valley to market. I knew he wanted us out, but I never thought he would stoop to this."

Melody remembered very little about the burial. The Matthews, their only neighbors in the valley besides the Winslows, had come; Mr. Matthews had helped Pa dig a hole up the hill west of the house where they buried Mark's body. Ma hadn't said a word to anyone since Mark's death; she stood mute at his graveside while Mr. Matthews read some scripture and said a few words Melody didn't remember. He closed by quoting, "The Lord gave, an' the Lord hath taken away; blessed be the name of the Lord."

At that Ma started to scream in a voice unlike any that Melody had ever heard. She threw her arms in the air shaking her fists and screaming at a stunned Mr. Matthews, "No! The Lord didn't take him away."

When Pa tried to quiet her, she just shouted more loudly, "I buried two babies an' was comforted that it was the will of my Lord, but not this time—not this time. The Lord didn't take Mark away from me. H. J. Winslow did, an' he must pay for it—he must!"

After they got Ma in the house and quieted her down

some, Pa told Melody to watch her mother and rode off on one of the Matthews' horses without telling anyone where he was going. They sat up waiting for him until the middle of the night, when a rider appeared outside their door leading a horse that carried her Pa slung over the saddle. She knew the other man was Marty Simpson, Winslow's foreman, because he had been to their place several times with Mr. Winslow, trying to convince her father that he should move up into the foothills out of their rangeland. Pa had refused, saying that the land up there was untillable.

Marty and Ma didn't speak until they had gotten Pa off the horse and into the house where they laid him on the same bed that had cradled Mark's body earlier that same day.

Ma broke the silence in a flat, emotionless voice. "OK, mister, tell me why yore bringin' my man home half dead."

"Mrs. Chaffin, I'm real sorry about this, but yore husband came lookin' fer trouble. He must have knowed that most everybody would be on roundup. I was on my way t' join the men, myself." He shifted his weight from foot to foot, twisting his hat in his big hands as he spoke. "Anyhow, he come int' our place shoutin' for H. J. t' come out, an' callin' him a murderer. When H. J. opened the door, Mr. Chaffin shot him in the shoulder with his rifle. I came out of the barn jest in time t' stop him from killin' my boss. I didn't have no time t' aim t' disarm him. I couldn't even see who it was. I jest shot an' he doubled over fallin' t' the ground." The man was clearly upset as he said, "I'm sorry, ma'am. I'm really sorry!"

Melody had never seen such hate, before, as she saw on her mother's face. Her usual soft voice was shaking with rage as she spit out, "Don't give me any of your 'I'm sorrys.' My only son was killed two days ago, an' now my husband will probably die because of you an' yore kind. Now there will be no one to keep this place goin'. We came here so we could get us some land to leave our boy. Thanks to yore Mr. Winslow, there ain't no boy t' leave it to."

"Please, Mrs. Chaffin, you have t' understand. We didn't even know yore boy was dead until yore husband showed up at our place. Our boys have been ridin' over this land on their roundup fer many years 'fore you folks ever came here. I'm sure they jest meant t' level a few fences. We . . . "

Ma interrupted him with a venom that made him realize she was not to be talked out of her hate. "Get out of my house this minute an' don't ever come back, or I'll have the pleasure of shuttin' you up permanent-like—lady or no!"

Two days later, they buried Pa beside Mark. Then Mr. Matthews took them in his buckboard all the way to the nearest stage that they rode to the train that eventually took them to St. Louis. Uncle Mark had taken them in, and it was behind his prosperous lady's dress shop that she had spent the rest of her childhood. She had never been so happy again as she had been in the open country. Although she grew to like St. Louis, very little else in her life was to her liking. Her mother had grown more bitter as the years wore on, and lately she had been barely sane. She would rave on and on about revenge.

"If I only had a son," she would cry, "he would avenge the murders of Pa and Mark. Oh, why didn't I have another son?"

Melody had hated herself for a long time because she

wasn't a boy. After her Uncle's death, she decided that maybe she should go back and see if she could do something about what had happened to her family. She wasn't sure what she could do, but somehow she hoped that if she could bring her mother news that H. J. Winslow had paid for what he had done, her mother would be better. Despite her fiancé's objections, she took the money her uncle had left her; leaving her mother with an aunt, she headed for what was now called Marysville. She used her mother's maiden name when she applied for the school-marm job, so no one would know who she was.

Walking through the ruins of her former home, she thought of what it would have looked like by now—of all the plans her folks had had for the place, and of their plans to leave the land to future generations of Chaffins. Instead there were no Chaffins left to carry on the family name. She didn't bother looking for the graves since they had left too hastily to put up markers. She had hoped the Matthewses might still be around and would remember where they were, but the Matthewses had sold out to Winslow two years before, when a dry year took care of their plans for the future.

Winslow was always popping up in her life to frustrate something or other. Well, she wasn't sure of the details yet, but she was sure that one way or another, she would get even with him—for everything.

So engrossed was she in her thoughts, as she came out of the house, that she didn't notice the two riders rapidly bearing down on her.

Three

Chad was enjoying the long ride to the ranch. Not liking the tack and style of riding preferred by his Eastern friends, he hadn't ridden much at college. This was where he belonged, there was no doubt about it. He loved this valley nestled in the Rocky Mountains—his father's valley which would someday be his. He wondered for the first time if he would run it the way his father would want him to.

He looked at Marty riding a little ahead of him, and a frown formed on his face. Had Marty changed so much, or was his memory clouded with boyhood hero worship? Marty had been his father's closest ally since before Chad was born, and when Chad was growing up, Marty had been like a second father to him. Actually, in many ways he had been closer to Marty than to his father. It hurt to see that Marty was getting old. He still sat straight and tall in the saddle, but his hair and whiskers were mostly grey, and his face held lines that shouldn't have been there yet. For the first time, Chad realized that his father would be getting older, too.

With each man deep in his own thoughts, the ride

passed quickly. They were comfortable enough together, even after the long separation, to ride along enjoying each other's company without a lot of idle chatter. As they topped the last small hill before the ranch, they both pulled up as if by common agreement.

Marty laid his reins across his horse's neck, crooked one leg around the saddle horn, and leisurely rolled himself a cigarette.

Chad got off Beau and stood regarding the huge spread. It hadn't changed much since he had last seen it—except for the fences everywhere. Most of the buildings stood as before, clustered around the two-storied white clapboard house that had been his mother's delight. Very proud of his aristocratic southern wife, H. J. had loved to surround her with the beautiful, expensive things she was used to. He and Marty had been content to live in a small log cabin, which was now the cook shack, until Mary Winslow had arrived. She had brought a lot of furniture from St. Louis with her, and every year she would go east or south returning with several wagons full of the latest things for herself and her house. There really was very little need for such a lavish house with no one around to impress but cowhands, but she had loved pretty things—and H. J. had loved her.

The difference between this house and the other buildings was a not-too-subtle reminder of the difference in lifestyles between the family and the hired hands. The bunkhouse was just a long row of rooms strung together that was home to the steady cowhands, the drifters who hired on for a season, and a constant stream of visiting cowhands from other parts of Winslow's far-flung empire. Most of these men never saw the interior of the main house. Marty was supposed to live in the house with the family, but he preferred a room in the bunkhouse. "I'm a cowhand, an' I like bein' 'round cowhands," he used to say.

"Marty, remember how I used to love to come and visit in the bunkhouse when I was kid? The smell of sweat, manure from the men's boots, and cigarette smoke was like a perfume to me. And how I loved the stories you guys used to tell! I learned a lot in that bunkhouse."

Marty laughed and said, "Yeah, like how t' whittle, an' play cards, an' a few words ya wouldn't have knowed otherwise."

Chad said with a grin, "Don't forget chewing and spitting. I got pretty good at that before Mom caught me at it. Was she mad!"

"As I recollect, that made her insist the time had come t' send ya away t' school. H. J. an' me had always figured the time would come, but we hadn't been ready t' lose you so soon. It was a hard time fer us both." The older man frowned as he remembered.

"It wasn't a very good time for me, either. I never would have made it through those first few years if I hadn't been able to come home a couple of times a year."

"How come ya stayed away so long this time?"

"By going to school summers, I was able to finish more quickly, and that was important to me." The young man swung back on Beau and said, "You know, every time I've come home I've seen some changes in the valley, but never like this time. I realize that I was gone longer; still, that doesn't account for everything. Marysville must be double its old size, and there seem to be homesteads around every bend. The only place that looks the same is ours—except for all these fences. I don't ever remember having to open a gate to get to the ranch before."

"Yeah, I recall when ya could ride clean 'cross the territory without openin' a single gate. As I told ya before, things are changin' an' not fer the better."

After that the two men rode in silence to the corral gate where Marty took the horses, telling Chad to go on in. Since this would be the first time Chad had been in the house since his mother's death, Marty figured he would want to be alone. Marty had even sent Rosie, the Winslow's long-time housekeeper, into town with the cowhands' cook.

In the house, Chad ambled through the rooms, taking in all the old familiar details. He was pleased to see that his father hadn't changed anything. Funny, neither his father nor he had really liked all the fancy things that his mother had crowded the house with, but somehow with her gone it was reassuring to find everything still there.

By the time Marty caught up with him, Chad was in his own room in the north corner of the house, searching through his drawers for something. Without looking up he said, "I'm looking for my Colt. You know, the one Dad gave me when I turned sixteen."

"I have it right here," Marty said handing the gun to Chad. "I cleaned it fer ya an' got some bullets jest in case you needed it. The new holster an' belt are a sort of comin' home an' graduation present from me."

"Thanks, Marty. It looks great." As he fastened the buckle and pulled the belt down to ride comfortably on his hips, he said, "Now I really feel at home. A man just doesn't feel right without his gun. Those Eastern dudes couldn't understand that. They called me 'cowboy' because I always wore my hat and boots, but they don't know what a real cowboy is."

"I weren't sure if you would be wearin' a gun, now that

yore a full-fledged lawyer."

As he checked his appearance in the full-length mirror, Chad laughingly said, "Even big-shot lawyers get shot at. Besides, it goes with the outfit. Don't you think? Say, when will cook be back with my things? After that long dusty ride, I could use a hot bath and some clean clothes."

"Before long. Since Rosie is with him, he won't go int' the saloon with the other fellars. She'll be hollerin' to get home." Marty started for the door. "I gotta git. Before supper, I want t' check out the corrals over at the ol' Matthews place, in case we want t' use them fer brandin' this year. I guess H. J. wrote you that Matthews finally sold the place t' us."

Chad picked up his hat and called after him, "Hold on a minute, I'll wait on that bath and ride over with you. I would like to get in on as much ranch business as I can after being gone for so long."

Marty smiled as Chad joined him. "I was hoping you'd say that. I didn't even unsaddle Beau."

The two men rode along without talking much, except an occasional remark about the countryside. After a while, they saw the remains of a log cabin in the distance.

Chad asked, "That isn't the Matthews place. Is it? It sure is run down."

Marty seemed a bit uneasy when he answered, "No, I think the family what lived there was named Chaffin. They left about eight years ago, an' Matthews sort of took over their land."

They spotted the horse standing outside the cabin at the same time. "What the heck?" said Marty.

At that moment a figure came out of the door and walked toward the horse. "Marty, it's a woman. Even in those men's clothes, you can tell that."

Melody looked up when Fortune whinnied and decided that the two men were too close for her to leave without being seen. So, she just stood and waited for them to ride over to her. She recognized Marty Simpson, even though he had aged some since she had last seen him, but she didn't know who the black-haired giant beside him was.

"Hey, lady, what're ya doin' here? And how did ya get through that fence yonder?" Marty asked.

Melody quickly decided this wasn't the time to display any hostility so she answered sweetly, "It was such a lovely afternoon that I was just doing some exploring around the area. Since I arrived in town about two months ago, I have not been able to explore much, and I do love to ride."

Chad got down and walked toward her; Marty stayed on his horse. She continued, "I hope I'm not bothering anybody. This place looked deserted, and I was just curious about it. I used to live in a log cabin when I was a little girl. By the way, I'm the new schoolteacher in town, Melody Grant."

Chad wiped his hand on his jeans before taking her outstretched one. Marty tipped his hat and said, "I'm Marty Simpson, foreman of the Winslow spread, and this here's Chad Winslow."

Marty was watching the pleasure on Chad's face as he held the young woman's hand. She was a pretty little thing, that was for sure. Her light hair gleamed in the last sunrays. It hung well below her waist and was caught back in a ribbon below her neck. Her hat hung from her neck by its strap. The men's clothes she wore couldn't disguise her full figure. It had been a long time since he had seen a woman so comely. Since he had first seen

Chad's mother, in fact.

Her sparkling blue eyes studied Chad as she said in a deep throaty voice, "Pleased to meet you, gentlemen. Tell me, is this part of the Winslow spread?"

Chad recovered his senses enough to answer, "Yes, this quarter section and the one just north of here were purchased a while back by my father. We were just on our way to the Matthews place to the north."

Marty interrupted. "You never did say how ya got through that fence yonder. I know there ain't no gate in it."

The woman smiled, lighting up her face, as she said, "Why, I jumped it, of course." She stepped into the stirrup and swung expertly into the saddle.

"Lady, you've gotta be kiddin'. I don't know many horses what could clear that fence, an' I ain't ever seen no woman what could stay on if it did," Marty challenged.

"Just watch, mister," Melody called over her shoulder. The beautiful long-legged horse took off at a dead gallop and never even hesitated before easily clearing the fence.

Marty and Chad watched with open mouths as the girl waved at them and quickly disappeared over a small hill.

Chad laughed at Marty. "I guess you have to eat your words, old buddy. That girl can really ride!"

"I gotta admit I ain't ever seen anything like that. That is some horse!"

"That is also some woman," muttered Chad, deep in his own thoughts.

Marty didn't especially like the way Chad looked, but then he was getting to the marrying age. H. J. was anxious for him to produce grandsons to insure that there would be Winslows around for generations to own his land. Still, they had just gotten Chad back after a long absence, and Marty wanted the boy to be interested mainly in the ranch for awhile yet. Grandchildren for the old man would come in time. "Come on, Chad. It'll be gettin' dark 'fore we're done if we don't get goin'."

When they got to the Matthews place, they checked the fences and corrals, finding them in fair shape, and then decided to see what condition the barn was in. As they walked up to the door, Chad kicked aside a board and heard the ominous buzz of a rattler. He instinctively jumped back, drew his gun and fired only to hit a board a couple of inches above the snake. Before he could fire again, Marty had drawn and blasted the snake's head off. Chad had forgotten how fast Marty was, but his thoughts were more on his own miss. "Blast it," he muttered under his breath.

Marty couldn't help but laugh—more at the look on Chad's face than anything else. He wasn't a man to brag about his shooting. It was just something that had to be done. "Yore draw ain't bad, but I reckon you could use a little practice on yore aim."

Chad didn't find the incident very funny. This country might be changing; it still wasn't any place for a man who couldn't shoot straight. He was going to have to polish up his skills.

Riding back to the house, Chad's mind was full of many things: what his dad was doing in Silver City, his need for some target practice, and most of all the blue eyes and creamy skin of the new schoolmarm. He was sure going to have to make a trip into town, soon.

Four

Back in town, Sam Farris grew restless behind his desk and decided to pay a visit to Sally's to see if anything was happening. By now the north end of town would be coming alive, and that usually meant news of some kind. As a husband and father, he hated all the noise and trouble these establishments caused; as a newsman, he was aware that they were his chief source of copy. Especially when Winslow's hands were in town. Of course, with Shorty in jail over at Silver City, one of the chief trouble-makers was out of the picture—at least until Winslow could spring him.

After checking out the other saloon and finding everything pretty much as usual, he sauntered into Sally's place where most of the noise was coming from. The smell of booze and cigarette smoke filled the air. There was hardly room to walk. He noticed more miners than usual in the crowd. Since most of the mines were located closer to Silver City, that was where the men usually went for their fun. There were always a few that found Marysville more congenial. Apparently, Sheriff Brady was running troublemakers out of Silver City, adding to the problems in Marysville. Their presence, and the sprinkling of cowhands from the smaller spreads in the valley mixed with Winslow's hands made Sam uneasy. The Winslow hands rarely fought among themselves, but the addition of outsiders could cause trouble.

Everything looked peaceful at the two faro games. Here and there brightly made-up girls were sitting at tables with half-drunk men, or holding them up on the dance floor while a fancily dressed dude embarrassed the piano. Sam elbowed his way to the bar and said to the barkeeper, "Hey there, Max. How about a beer?" When Max set the foamy drink in front of him, Sam asked, "Anything interesting happening in here tonight?"

"Nah, Mr. Farris. A few more customers than usual. That's 'bout all."

At the mention of Sam's name, a stocky, grimy man shoved aside the two men who were standing between him and Sam, and stood face to face with Sam. His eyes were watery from too much whiskey, and his words were slurred as he gnashed his teeth and said, "Yore Sam Farris, the big mouth newsman, ain't ya?"

Sam met his glare with a level glance. "Yes. What does it matter to you?"

"I'm Frank Smith an' Shorty's my friend. I don't like ya callin' him a murderer. Who cares 'bout a stinkin' ol' sheepman, anyhow? The fewer of 'em—the better."

"Frankly, I'm surprised that you can even read the paper." Sam laughed and instantly knew he had made a big mistake.

A strange, almost animal look came into the other man's eyes as he swung and punched Sam in the jaw. To Frank's surprise, the blow only swayed Sam a little, and he threw a counter-punch that landed squarely on

Frank's jaw, sending him sprawling backwards across a table. Several of his friends pushed him back toward Sam while yelling encouragement. They had been waiting for this fight, and they were all sure that Frank could easily wipe up the floor with the skinny, pale Farris. They soon realized their mistake, for Sam Farris was a strong man who had learned to fight at a young age in an eastern tenement. As Frank came at him bellowing, Sam caught him by his shirt front and easily threw him over the bar. Frank landed on Max, momentarily stunning both men. At that the girls started to scream, miners began to hit cattlemen, Winslow cowhands began to hit non-Winslow cowhands, tables were overturned, and the Faro dealers and piano player retreated to the back office.

Some of Frank's friends came at Farris only to be met by some of the ranchers who considered Sam their friend. A couple of men got close to Sam, but he managed to brace himself against the bar, and kicking out with his full weight, knocked them backwards into a group of miners who engaged them in a fist fight. Frank recovered some and started around the bar after Sam, who swung around in time to punch Frank hard in the stomach, dropping him to his knees. Someone hit Sam from behind and his legs started to sag. Two others jumped him and he fell beneath their weight. Just before he blacked out, he thought to himself, "When I came looking for a story, I didn't expect to be in it."

Sam came to, face down in the dirt outside the saloon, wondering who had thrown him out. There was blood running down his face, and he couldn't move without wincing from the pain, especially in his chest. There still seemed to be some fighting going on inside, and every once in a while another body would hit the dirt around him as the bouncers began to clear out the bar. He staggered to his feet with the help of a post and slowly, gingerly started home, which seemed like an eternity away.

Lenore was beginning to get worried about both Sam and Melody before she heard a faint knock on the back door. She wondered who it could be, since only family used the back door, and they wouldn't knock. Later, she wondered why, but she took Sam's rifle down from the rack beside the door before opening the door. The sight of Sam with blood all over him made her drop the rifle and cry, "My God, what happened to you?"

Sam started to walk in the house, but his knees gave out, and he sagged against the door frame. Fortunately, Melody came in just then, and the two women managed to help him up the stairs and on the bed. After they had washed the blood and dirt off his face and hands, they could see that he was bruised badly but didn't have any major wounds.

When he was revived enough to talk to them, Lenore repeated her question. Sam told them what he could remember, mentioning as few details as possible, because he could see the pain on Lenore's face when he mentioned getting hit.

"Those damn roughnecks, they'll fight over anything," Lenore said.

Sam had to laugh at her unusual use of profanity, and it made him wince with pain. "Now Lenore, what kind of language is that for a Christian lady to use?"

"I don't care. You should hear the language that is going around in my head, if you think that's bad. I'll just bet H. J. Winslow himself put them up to it. Especially since that man mentioned Shorty Johnson. Didn't you say Winslow went to Silver City to get him off? I tried to tell you that you would antagonize him with your editorial about Shorty. This is probably just a warning. Next time they'll do something worse!"Lenore said with tears in her eyes.

"I don't think Winslow had anything to do with this. Whenever he doesn't like something I've printed, he either tells me himself or sends Simpson in to see me. This was just the whiskey talking. Those men love to fight, and if they hadn't had me around, they would have jumped on someone else. I doubt if they'll even remember what happened tomorrow."

Melody spoke for the first time. "I agree with Lenore, Sam. Winslow is capable of anything, and anyone who crosses him ends up hurt—and hurt bad! He uses his cowhands to do his dirty work, but it's still his doing. You had better take care to stay away from him and his bunch from now on."

Sam looked closely at her flushed face and said, "I didn't know you knew Winslow that well."

"Well, I do. I know him far better than I would like to."

The venom in her voice when she spoke Winslow's name surprised both Lenore and Sam. They started to ask her more, but she left the room.

Forgetting all about her supper, she went into her own room. She was so angry she couldn't even sleep. She knew that somehow Winslow had to be stopped before he ruined any more lives. For the first time, she could understand why her mother had always cried for a son to get revenge.

What could she do? She could ride as well as any man, she was sure of that, and she could fire a rifle fairly well. That wasn't enough, probably, but it would have to do. No one else seemed willing to do much more than complain about the Winslows. Sam was trying to fight them in his own way, but she didn't think it was enough. Besides, Sam wouldn't be able to do much for a while, anyway.

As she lay there thinking, she wondered about this Chad fellow. Was he as ruthless as the senior Winslow? Probably, although Sam had said that he had been away at school quite awhile, which could have changed him. He certainly didn't look like a selfish, grasping person. He really was very nice-looking with curly black hair and eyes that were as blue as hers. If he had been anyone else, she might have . . . keep your mind on your business, she reprimanded herself. She would have to get to know him, but not for social reasons. After all, who could give her a better view of Winslow's business and the lay-out of the ranch? What good that would do her, she wasn't sure yet. With those thoughts, she finally went to sleep, only to dream about her old home.

The next morning she awoke to find it snowing. She had forgotten about the sudden spring snowstorms that often came to blanket this area. Usually she loved the snow; today, it just made her feel frustrated. She had things to do, and now she wouldn't be able to go anywhere until the sun melted the snow. She didn't want to be so easily tracked. For the next two days, she kept busy helping Lenore with Sam.

Sam insisted that he could go back to work, but when he tried to get up he almost passed out from the pain around his ribs. As much as he hated to admit it, it would be awhile before he was up to walking much. He wondered if someone had kicked him, but it didn't really matter much how it had happened. He had taken the Oleson boy on as an apprentice, and Sam was sure he could set the type and run off the paper. Lenore brought him some things from his desk, and he wrote up the stories that needed printing. Lenore tried to talk him out of writing about the brawl at Sally's for fear that it would just stir up more trouble.

"What if it had been some other man? Think about this—an ordinary citizen isn't even safe going in for a quick drink after work. I think the rest of this valley ought to know about this. I wouldn't hesitate to print it if it had happened to someone else, and I'm not going to hesitate just because it was me," he replied stubbornly.

He ran a late edition on Saturday which contained the story under the headline: "Editor Assaulted in Sally's Saloon." He just stated the bare facts, saving his comments for his editorial which restated his belief that the town needed a full-time law enforcement officer. He said again that theirs was the only town of its size in the territory without any peace officer. He didn't mention Winslow by name since he figured everyone knew by now that Winslow ran the valley his way, and didn't want any law interfering.

Five

Sunday, on his way home from Silver City, H. J. stopped in town to pick up Saturday's paper, thinking there would be a piece in it about Chad's homecoming. Before leaving Marysville, he had told Farris to write an article about it. He also figured there might be something else about Shorty. What he hadn't figured on was seeing the front page taken up with a story about Farris getting himself beaten up. He just glanced at the headline without taking the time to read the whole paper, because he was anxious to get home and see his son.

He had sorely missed that boy, especially since his mother's passing. It would be good to see him again, and H. J. could use his help right now. He was beginning to realize that having a lawyer in the family might be to his advantage. Wanting his son to take over the ranch eventually, he had felt that Chad had spent too much time away from it already. However, Mary had wanted Chad to be a lawyer; she was the one person that H. J. never could say no to.

It had taken him longer to get home than he had figured

because of the snow. "Blasted country," he muttered to no one, "The trees are already budded out, an' it starts t' snow again." He had very little love for this area of the country. He was only here because he had been sure that he could make a great deal of money—which he had. It had stopped snowing in the night, and now the sun was shining warmly on his face. The snow would melt quickly. It was usually like that with these late snows. Just enough to make him late, which he didn't like. The weather always frustrated him, because it was the only thing he wasn't able to control—until lately, anyway. It seemed like everything was getting out of his control lately.

He was so deep in his thoughts that he almost rode past the main house. Marty called out, "Hey, H. J., ya jest passin' through, or are ya come t' stay a spell?"

His boss grunted and stopped his horse. Giving the reins to Marty as he stepped down, he said, "Get Ed t' take care of my horse an' you come in the house. I'll tell you about my trip. Is the boy inside?"

"Yeah, he's writin' a letter t' some college friends."

From the front window, Chad watched his father cross the yard toward the house. He has aged a lot in these last few years, Chad thought. He was heavier than before, even though he had always been a big man. His face wore an annoyed look, and there were brown splotches over his face and hands. His hair wasn't as grey as Marty's, but it was receding rapidly from his forehead. Chad noticed it when his Dad removed his hat and hung it on the hat rack in the hall. Remembering how his mother had nagged at them both for wearing hats in the house, Chad smiled.

Chad gave H. J. a hug and said, "It's about time you came home to welcome your favorite son."

The old man's face lit up at the greeting. "Are you ever

a sight for sore eyes. Boy, I've really missed you."

"I've missed you too, Dad. I wish I had been here with you when Mom died."

H. J. grew silent at the mention of his wife. He didn't answer until they were both seated by the fire in the parlor drinking the coffee that Rosie had brought. Then he said, "I know, son. I wanted you here too. She got sick so fast that she was gone before I had time t' let you know. I figured it would take you so long t' get here, there was no use tellin' you until after she was buried. Have you been to her grave yet?"

Chad nodded. "Yes, I went back there yesterday. It is a beautiful spot."

Marty walked in then, and H. J. abruptly changed the subject. "Would you believe, they are actually plannin' on hangin' Shorty? I've never been so mad in my life as I was at that idiot of a sheriff at Silver City. I didn't even get t' see Shorty. That sheriff claimed that there was some talk about lynching him, so he was sent t' the territorial prison to wait trial." The more he talked the louder his voice rose. "Did I tell you that the man he shot was only a sheepman? Can you imagine? Used t' be 'round here that a cattleman would 've been rewarded for riddin' the territory of a stinkin' sheepman."

"I guess you've been lucky there's never been any sheep in Basin River Valley," remarked Chad.

"Lucky, hell! There aren't any sheep here, because I haven't allowed it. This mess is one of the reasons. Every time they come int' a place there's trouble—every time. Anyway, tomorrow I want you t' ride over t' the prison an' see Shorty. He's goin' t' need you t' defend him."

Chad studied his Dad for quite awhile before answering, "I don't know if I can defend him if he really did kill someone. I believe everyone—even cattlemen—has to obey the law. Times are changing."

H. J.'s face turned red with rage as he shouted at his son, "I don't need you t' tell me times are changin'—I can see that. But none of my boys are goin' t' hang because of no blamed sheepman. Besides, I should get some good out of all that money I've spent gettin' you through school."

Marty, hoping to calm H. J. down, asked him about the paper he had brought in with him. H. J. picked it up and threw it at Marty. "Here," he shouted, "read it yourself."

Marty quietly picked up the paper that was scattered over the rug and started to glance over the front page, but H. J. said impatiently, "No, read it out loud. I didn't get a chance t' read more than just the headline."

Marty read about the fight at Sally's which started H. J. cursing again. "What the hell does that fool expect, saunterin' int' my saloon askin' a lot of fool questions? Any jackass ought t' know better than that. Those men are all friends of Shorty's an' Farris has been sayin' he should be hanged. Read the editorial. I'll bet it's a beaut!"

Marty read the editorial, glancing up every once in awhile to see how his boss was taking it. Every sentence or two brought a new volley of "damned fool" or "stupid jackass" but little else. When Marty had finished, H. J. stood up and started pacing the room. From long experience, Marty knew that H. J. paced like that only when he was so angry that he couldn't sit still. Not liking to be around H. J. when he was like that, Marty muttered something about seeing about some horses and left the room.

Chad had sat silently through all the reading and cursing and just watched his father. He couldn't understand why the town shouldn't have a sheriff, but he knew his Dad well enough to know that he hadn't better question his judgement on anything—at least until he knew more about the situation. He felt the same way about the Shorty business. He wouldn't defend a guilty man just because his father told him to, but he would save his decision until he had seen the man and talked to the sheriff at Silver City.

"Are you sure you want me to go over to the capital and Silver City? I'm just beginning to feel at home again, and here you are sending me away."

His father stopped pacing and came over to where Chad sat. He put his hand on his son's shoulder and said, "I'm sorry, son, that I got so riled up, but it's probably for the best that you found out what's happenin' round here right off. Someday this will be your valley, if we can keep the outsiders from takin' everything away from us."

"I've seen the fences everywhere, and I know how determined you were to keep the open rangeland. It must have taken some doing to get you to put up fences."

The anger began to show in H. J.'s face again, as he said, "Yore damn right, it did. Those fences meant surrender t' me, an' that is as far as I will allow the Winslows t' be pushed. Marty an' I were the first white men in this valley, an' except for a couple of homesteaders, we were the only outfit around 'til the stage came through. Now that the railroad is puttin' a line through the valley, you can bet there will be a lot more people comin' in."

Chad spoke very calmly so he wouldn't rile his father. "It's a big valley. Don't you think it could hold a few more people?"

"Sure, as long as they were cattlemen who would leave things the way they are."

"Well, I can tell you here is one man who looks forward to having a train close enough that I don't ever have to take a stagecoach again. What a lousy way to travel."

H. J. laughed in spite of himself. He slapped Chad on the back and said, "I know what you mean. That's the reason I always ride my horse t' Silver City. Anything is better than bein' pounded around in a stage. Anyway, I hope you won't be travelin' much now that you are home. If you are still determined t' practice law instead of runnin' this ranch, we can probably find an office for you in Marysville."

"You and Marty will be running this ranch for a long time yet, and I can keep an eye on the operations and still have a law practice. There can't be that much business for a lawyer in these parts—not yet, anyway."

"I know one man who can use your services right now, Shorty Johnson. You'll go over t' Silver City an' talk t' that nitwit sheriff tomorrow."

Chad noticed that his father hadn't made the last a question but a statement of fact—almost like an order. It was a habit that had irritated him as a kid; it didn't suit him much now, either. Deciding to ignore his irritation, Chad asked, "How long will it take me?"

"If you leave early tomorrow, you can be in Silver City well before supper, see the sheriff and get a good rest. The hotel there has a good dinin' room. Then the next day you could take the train t' the capital, see Shorty an' be back in Silver City that night. You should be home that next night. So you would be gone only about three days, unless you have t' wait around for that damn trial. Do you want t' take one of the boys with you just in case you run int' some kind of trouble? I don't think Marty should go because he will be startin' spring roundup in the morning.

The men work better when he's around."

"It doesn't matter. I'll probably be better off alone. No one knows me over there so I should be able to get in and out of town without anyone noticing me," Chad said as he rose from his chair. "I have some things I would like to look up in my books, if you'll excuse me."

That evening, Chad went out to the bunkhouse to see Marty. As he entered the first room, he saw several of the hands engaged in a poker game, a couple were whittling by the stove, and several more were just sitting and swapping stories. One of the men at the poker table called to him, "Hey, Chad, how 'bout a game? Let's see if ya really learned anythin' useful at yore fancy college."

Chad smiled but declined. He knew only about three of the men in the room. Most of the others were either drifters newly hired on, or regulars who had joined the outfit while he was away. Although they all knew him, he didn't know them, and he had long ago learned not to play cards with strangers. Besides, he had other things on his mind as he walked through the adjoining bunkroom where the men slept, and rapped on the door in the far wall.

Marty's voice told him to come in. When he saw who it was, Marty sat up on the bed and said quietly, "Close the door, son."

Chad sat down on the only chair. "You know, you ought to live in the big house with the old man and me. We would love your company, and this place stinks."

Marty laughed, making the wrinkles in his face more noticeable. "I seem t' remember ya sayin' the bunkhouse odors were like perfume to ya."

"All right, so I've grown prissy in my adulthood, but you know what I mean. You are more than just a hired hand. This place should be half yours. Your ability with horses and cattle, not to mention the way you handle the men, is what has made this spread a success."

A frown crossed Marty's face as he said, "Nah, I'm jest a cowhand. Yore Dad is the brains an' runs all the business. If it weren't for his business sense, there wouldn't be no ranch, or cows and horses fer me to work with. Besides, I tried t' sleep in the big house after yore mother died in order t' keep the ol' man company, but I 'bout went crazy. I'm happy right here, an' yore ol' man knows it." The look on his face made it clear to Chad that the subject was closed. "Now, what're ya doin' here? I'm sure ya didn't come t' tell me I should move."

"No, I didn't. You know that I am going to Silver City tomorrow, and I wanted to know a few things before I left. I figured you could give me a straight answer without getting so fired up like Dad did this afternoon."

Marty just nodded; so Chad went on, "First, tell me what you think happened in town between this Farris and Frank. Did the boys say anything about it to you?"

Marty thought for a minute before he answered, "Well, I wasn't there, as you know, but I know both of the men. I've talked t' Sam Farris a few times 'bout things he wrote in that paper of his. He seems t' be a nice enough fellow, he jest don't think like a cowman. Every little thing that happens 'round here, he blames on our outfit. As for Frank, he's a troublemaker an' has been from the moment he got here. He loves t' stir the other men up an' git 'em fightin'—someone else or each other—he don't care. He jest loves t' fight which I can't understand because he ain't much good at it. I won't hire him again, if I have anything t' say about it. In fact, I wouldn't be surprised but what he don't make it through roundup."

Chad leaned toward him and asked, "Did you hear

anything the night the fight took place?"

Marty laughed as he remembered. "Most of the men barely made it home that night. Why, some of 'em were brung home tied 'cross their saddles; so there was very little talk of any kind that night. The next mornin', they all looked like death warmed over, an' most couldn't remember too much what happened. By afternoon, they begun t' laugh an' kid each other 'bout this fight. Frank has been the brunt of most of their jokin'. Farris must have made him look like a fool, an' some of the others took Farris on. My guess is it'll be a long time 'fore Frank ever forgives Farris fer makin' him look bad in front of the other men."

"Is Frank really a friend of Shorty's? Frankly, I never liked Shorty much and I find it hard to believe that he ever had many friends."

"I doubt Shorty ever had any real friends. I reckon Frank jest feels like yore ol' man does, that bein' one of Winslow's hands makes ya better than most—especially sheepmen."

Chad looked at Marty very closely and asked, "How about you? How do you feel about what Shorty did?"

Marty spit in the general direction of the spittoon near the foot of the bed. He looked straight into Chad's eyes and said quietly, "I always feel 'bout these things jest like the ol' man does."

Figuring he had gotten all the information he was going to get from Marty, Chad got up and walked to the door. "Would you have the cook fix me up some jerky and sourdough biscuits to take with me tomorrow? I'll be riding most of the day, and Rosie's dinners are too darn dainty for me."

Marty grinned, and the two men said goodnight.

Chad was stopped on his way out of the bunkhouse by

a grimy looking man a little older than the usual cowboy. "Ya gonna git Shorty off? I see the whole thing, an' it weren't his fault."

Chad looked at Frank for a minute, then deciding he couldn't get much information out of him, just said, "I'll see what I can do," and left.

Six

Monday morning, Chad left the ranch just as the sun was coming up. Since he intended to make a stop in Marysville, he wanted to get an early start. He loved this time of day. Even in the East, he had always been up long before the others and would walk around the campus, savoring the time alone. He watched the sun rise over the mountains and fell in love with them all over again. He had missed those mountains almost as much as he had missed his family, and it was good to be back, even if he did feel that there was big trouble coming—bigger trouble than his father knew.

When he arrived in town, he rode to the newspaper office where he was told that Mr. Farris was still recuperating at home. He decided not to go to the Farris house since he didn't know them at all. Riding out of town, he spotted the schoolhouse off the road and thought he could probably get some information there, as the boy had told him Miss Grant was staying with the Farris family. Anyway, talking to her was bound to be more pleasant than talking to Farris. She was a very pleasant woman, indeed. She was even more beautiful than he had remembered. The prim black dress that she wore only accented her charm. It showed off her tiny waist and full bosom to great advantage, and the dark color made her eyes look bluer and her skin whiter. Her hair had been braided and twisted around some way on top of her head. Looking at her, he thought of how she would look with all that lovely golden hair falling loose around her face.

However, his arrival was a source of irritation to Miss Grant. First, it made the children giggle; she hated giggling, even from children. More than that, she didn't like the quick flash of pleasure she had felt when his tall frame appeared in the doorway.

He flashed her a smile and asked, "Can I have a word with you, Miss Grant?"

Melody spoke in what she considered her sternest voice and said to the children, "Everyone work on reading. I will be just outside, so no fooling around."

Knowing that she wasn't really very stern, the children continued to giggle and whisper about her caller.

Chad closed the door to the classroom, leaving them alone in the small entry. He thought for just a moment that really being alone with her would be a very nice experience, but then he remembered why he was there. "I'm sorry to interrupt your class. I'll only keep you a moment."

Melody was also very aware of being alone with him in a small area. Moving as far away from him as possible, she flushed a little, forgetting her irritation. "That's all right," she said in a low throaty voice that had been known to drop strong men to their knees. "What can I do for you, Mr. Winslow?"

"I'm on my way out of town on business, and I wanted to talk to Mr. Farris, who I understand is still laid up. I would like to say that my father and I deeply regret the incident that put him in bed."

A momentary flash of anger burned in Melody's eyes as she asked, "Did your father say that or is it your idea?"

Chad was taken back both by her question, and by the fact that the anger only made her more appealing to him. "We are both sorry it happened." That, he was sure, was the truth.

His evasive answer didn't fool Melody, but at least she had to admit that he did seem genuinely sorry. Maybe, he wasn't like his father. She hated to admit it, but she hoped he wasn't. "Well, I'll tell Mr. Farris that you came by and give him that message. Is there anything else?"

"Yes, I wanted to ask him a couple of questions. Since you have been staying with his family, I thought perhaps he had discussed some of these things at home."

"Like what?"

"What information does he have about Shorty Johnson, and where did he get it?"

Melody considered a moment and then answered, "I can only tell you what was in the paper, and you can get a back issue at the news office, if there isn't one around your father's place."

Chad couldn't miss the way she almost spit the words "your father" out. He wondered what this lovely young woman could have against his father after only being in the valley two months, but he didn't know her well enough to ask. "Very well, Miss Grant, I'll check at the paper. Better still, I'll be back in three or four days; perhaps by then Mr. Farris will be up to talking to me. Thank you for your time."

He touched the brim of his hat and left her standing alone, sorry she had allowed herself to be so sarcastic. If she intended to use his friendship, she would have to be more careful. She hoped that she would see him when he returned from Silver City, where she was sure he was headed, even if he hadn't said so. Sam had said he was a lawyer. He was probably going to try to get Shorty Johnson off.

Deciding to wait until his return trip to check at the paper, Chad rode on south toward Silver City. It had been a long time since he had been this way. At one time, Silver City had been the nearest town to the ranch; they had done a lot of trading there. Therefore, he wasn't totally unfamiliar with the way, and the stage route was clearly etched in the muddy road. He could have taken the stage, but he liked to ride alone. He planned on leaving Beau in town and taking the train to the capital.

It was a long ride, and Chad felt the need to get off several times and walk a bit. He hadn't spent the whole day on horseback since he had gone on a cattle drive one year when he was still in his teens. He had really enjoyed it. If it hadn't been for his mother, he knew he would have been content to grow up just like Marty. At first, she had been the only one who wanted him to be a lawyer, but as he studied, he found that he enjoyed law. He figured that he could be a lawyer part time and still get in on some of the ranch work. Actually, he considered himself pretty lucky; he could pick and choose what he wanted to do. After all, riding herd on a bunch of cattle day after day was a boring, tiring job. The exciting life of the cowboy was something created by writers for Eastern readers—reality was different.

Even though it was tiring, he was enjoying the solitary ride. He liked being alone which had been hard to do at college. Except for his early morning walks, it seemed there was always someone around wanting to talk. This was the first time he had been totally alone since he had gotten back, and making the most of it, he was in no hurry to get to Silver City.

Around noon, he stopped by a small creek and ate the jerky and biscuits, washing it down with water from his canteen. He would have liked a cup of coffee, but since he would be in town most of the time he was gone, he hadn't wanted to pack along cooking gear. He would get a hot meal and plenty of coffee when he got to town.

Since the incident with the snake, he had been practicing a great deal with his gun. So, when he spied a downed tree branch about fifty feet away, he drew and fired at it. After replacing the five bullets and making sure the empty chamber was under the firing pin, he slid the gun back into his holster, swung back into the saddle, and said to his horse, "Well, Beau, that's not too bad for someone who hasn't handled a gun in a long time. Three hits out of five doesn't make me an expert, but it's coming back to me."

It was nearly suppertime before he caught his first glimpse of Silver City. Situated southwest of Basin River Valley, it was the largest town in the county. A few years back, gold and silver had been discovered in the mountains near here, causing the town to spring overnight from a small trading post to a boomtown full of miners, cattlemen, sheepherders, homesteaders and businessmen, legal and otherwise, who made their money off the other men. In many ways, even with a sheriff, it was more open than Marysville, simply because there were more people to get into trouble and more places to get into it. Although it wasn't dark yet, the saloons, hurdy-gurdy dance halls, gambling house, and brothels were all lit up and doing a lively business, judging by the din that permeated the evening air.

Chad spotted the livery stable where he arranged to have Beau cared for. After asking directions to the sheriff's office and the Bailey Hotel, he decided to eat first since he didn't know how long he would be at the sheriff's office. In the hotel dining room, he ate a huge steak, fried potatoes and biscuits; and he drank several cups of thick, hot coffee. Feeling more up to what he figured was likely to be an unpleasant encounter, he made his way down the rough board sidewalk to the sheriff's office.

A young man, only two or three years older than Chad, greeted him as he entered the office. Chad would have thought he was the deputy except for the sheriff's badge prominently displayed on his chest. As tall as Chad and several pounds heavier, he wore a suit that gave him the appearance of a gambler rather than a peace officer. His thick black hair was straight, reaching almost to his shoulders; he sported an incredible mustache. Even in his office, he wore his gunbelt with a fancy gun unlike any Chad had seen before.

The young man rose and extended his hand, but his voice held a challenge as he said, "I'm Sheriff Brady. What can I do for you, stranger?"

Chad had the immediate impression that this man was far from the idiot his father believed him to be. Chad said, "I was wondering if I could get some information about the Shorty Johnson case."

Brady indicated a chair for Chad to sit in and after returning to his own chair, asked, "Are you a reporter or maybe one of those fool writers out to make a folk hero out of another murderer?"

Chad smiled as he shook his head. "No, I'm a lawyer who's only interested in the legal aspects of the case—

nothing else."

Brady studied Chad for quite awhile before he answered. Then he said, "I don't remember gettin' your name."

"Chad Winslow."

The sheriff's expression never changed, but his voice got lower as he asked evenly, "You any relation to H. J.?"

For the first time in his life, Chad felt at a disadvantage answering yes to that question.

Brady said with annoyance, "Well, I'll say one thing for you—you sure have a lot of gall. I told your ol' man not two days back that Shorty was at the territorial prison, and that is where I expect him to stay until he's hanged. I have enough trouble keepin' some order in this town without worryin' about the sheepmen lynchin' him or some of your ol' man's boys tryin' to spring him."

"I can understand your problems, but I am a lawyer who has been taught that every man is entitled to counsel. I knew that Shorty wasn't here, but I figured you could tell me what happened as well as anyone else. I'm only here to get some information. If I find out Shorty is guilty, I doubt if I will be able to bring myself to defend him. I believe a man has to obey the law—even a cattleman."

Brady relaxed a little at Chad's well-chosen words. He even smiled a little as he said, "Easy to see why you're a lawyer. You've got the glib tongue. Okay, I'll tell you what happened the best I know.

"Johnson rode in here a couple weeks back with some drifter named Frank Smith—probably an alias. I don't know why these fellows can't be more original. It's gettin' so every time I meet a Smith, I start checkin' wanted posters. Anyway, I don't know where they came from, but they were headed for the Winslow spread to hire on for the season. I understand Shorty has worked for your ol' man before. It seems they hung around the Longhorn for two or three hours drinkin' whiskey and swappin' lies with some of the cowhands recently hired on around these parts. In the meantime, the three Martinez brothers, who are sheepherders to the west of here, came into the saloon, mosied over to the bar, and ordered three beers. That much everyone agrees on. From there on, there are two different stories." He leaned back in his chair and braced his feet against his desk. Chad noticed that his boots, although dusty, didn't look like they saw much hard use.

"There usually are two different stories," Chad said.

The sheriff nodded before going on. "According to Shorty and Frank, the sheepherders became belligerent all of a sudden for no reason and started swingin' at them. Then one of the men came at Shorty with a knife, and Shorty shot him in self defense." He paused to let that story sink in before he said, "According to the Martinez brothers, and the only non-involved person in the room who would admit to seein' the shootin', Shorty and Frank began makin' insultin' remarks about the stink, and so on, the moment the brothers walked in. These men have heard it all before, and not wantin' a fight, they ignored them. The cowhands soon grew tired of being ignored and started punchin' them. Apparently, the sheepherders were moppin' up the floor with the two cowhands. The youngest one knocked Shorty to the floor; Shorty lost his temper and shot the man clean through the chest. If the dead man had a knife, I never found it, and I was there right after it happened. In fact, I was on my way to the saloon when I heard the shot. When I walked in, everyone was busy mindin' his own business except the Martinezes, who were tryin' to get some response from their dead brother."

"Then you would testify that in your opinion, Shorty killed an unarmed man." Chad had been afraid that was the case; still, he didn't like to hear it.

"That's what I intend to do. As far as I'm concerned, that's what happened."

"Is there anyone else who will testify to that?" Chad asked.

"The Martinez brothers, and a new saloon girl, who has not yet learned to be deaf and blind when something like that happens."

Chad got up and started toward the door before he said, "Thanks for your time. You don't mind if I ask around the saloon, do you?"

"Well, I won't stop you, but I would prefer you go easy. There's a lot of bad feelin' on both sides around here right now. Some of the cattlemen don't like one of their kind being hanged, especially because of a sheepman. The rest of the town seems to be angry about the shootin'. I don't think anyone cares much for Shorty one way or the other."

After finding the Longhorn Saloon, Chad ambled in and up to the bar. The bartender agreed to tell him what had happened after Chad told him who he was. He said, "I've knowed Marty Simpson awhile; he's a heck of a man."

Chad smiled at the man's praise of Marty. Encouraged, the bartender went on. "Frankly, I wondered why he would hire th' likes of that Johnson feller or his crony. Mind you, I don't care much fer sheepmen, myself, but I cain't say much for a man what'll shoot an unarmed man.

It jest ain't right. That's all."

"Do you know the Martinezes?" Chad asked.

"I've seen them in here a few times, an' they never bothered no one. Jest kept t' themselves. After awhile, even the local cowhands left 'em alone." He paused and looked around, as if for approval, before adding, "I figure they are goin' t' hang Shorty anyway; so it might as well be over an' done. Then, maybe we can all get back t' normal 'round here."

As they talked, a small group of cowhands had formed around Chad, and they seemed to agree with most of what the bartender had said. One of them added, "Ain't none o' us gonna rat on our own kind, but we don't cotton much t' shootin' an unarmed man, either. We ain't never had no trouble with the Martinez bunch afore. Now, they're all carryin' guns. Mark my word, there'll be more trouble over this." There were several grunts of agreement from the other men.

Chad talked to the saloon girl, who repeated the story that Brady had given him. Deciding there wasn't anymore to do there, he started back to the hotel. Then, he remembered the bartender telling him that the Martinezes had insisted on calling a priest before they would remove their brother's body. Remembering that there was a small Catholic chapel on the other side of town, he walked toward where he thought it would be. At one time, it had been an Indian mission; with most of the Indians shipped away, it had fallen into disuse until the influx of Mexicans and others with a Catholic background had swelled its congregation again. Seeing a light coming from a window in the rear, he knocked and was bid enter by an elderly *padre*. The father was pleasant and sympathetic to his problem of finding a defense for Shorty.

"God knows, I always try to be forgiving, but the Martinez family are God-fearing people, who never made any trouble for anyone that I know of. Raul, who was shot, had five small children, who are fatherless just because some man objected to his occupation and probably his nationality. I didn't see the fight, you realize, but if I were asked to testify, I would have to say that I have never seen a Martinez carry a knife or a gun in town. At least, not until after this terrible tragedy."

Not being able to think of anything more to say, Chad said goodnight, and walked back toward the hotel. Besides dreading his visit to the prison, his mind was full of the things he had heard tonight. He didn't even hear the men approaching behind him until one called out, "Hey you, Gringo."

Hand on his gun, he whirled around to face two short, stocky Mexican men with rifles pointed at his belly.

Seven

The older of the two men spoke in a heavy accent. "Why you been askin' questions about my brother's killer?" he asked, pushing the rifle barrel against Chad's stomach.

Before Chad could answer, a third man stepped out of the shadows and said in a menacing voice, "I'll tell you what he wants. He is trying to get someone to say that the cowman is innocent so he can get him free."

As the Mexican spoke, Chad was surrounded by a dozen other men, all armed and all wearing angry looks on their dark faces. Chad could feel his stomach tighten as they slowly began to encircle him. He knew that he couldn't say anything to make the situation better, and he sure couldn't shoot it out with all these men.

There was a lot of muttering and cursing among the men, and one said, "If you want to get him off so bad, how about you takin' his place. We could hang you right now!"

"Si," said another, "I heard him tell the men in the saloon that he's a Winslow. Winslows kill sheepmen—why can't sheepmen kill a Winslow?"

A voice behind Chad said, "It looks like he is the only

person what can get that Shorty fellow free. All we have to do is get rid of him, and Shorty is done for."

Then, one of the men, who had taken Chad's gun, shoved the hard barrel into his back and said, "Better get along here, Gringo. We'll tell you when to stop."

The man with the rifle on him stepped aside, and Chad was pushed along by the angry men, who were getting louder by the minute. Several times, he heard someone say, "Let's hang him." When they started to turn into an alley, Chad thought how stupid it was for him to be in this position because of a man he didn't even like. Suddenly, he was startled by the sound of a familiar voice.

"Goin' somewhere?" Sheriff Brady asked. He stood in the middle of the alley with his gun drawn and pointed at the front of the group. Behind him stood three deputies carrying shotguns. The Mexicans stopped; Brady said to the one who had Chad's gun, "I think you better give the man back his gun since you won't be needin' it. You all best be gone before I have time to think about what you may have been up to and decide to arrest you. If I see any of you in town with a gun again, I'll let you spend some time in my jail."

The man handed Chad his gun and said to Brady, "We just want someone to pay for my brother's murder."

The sheriff said impatiently, "I've told you before, Shorty Johnson will hang for that. You have to leave the law to me. You're just goin' to make more trouble for your family and friends if you don't leave this thing alone. Go home and let me do my job."

A great sense of relief washed over Chad as the men began to leave, muttering to themselves. He replaced his gun, and stuck out his hand toward Brady. "Thanks, I thought for a minute there I was a goner."

Ignoring Chad's hand, the sheriff said, "Don't thank me for doin' my job. I get paid. Just remember I warned you about askin' too many questions. You're lucky I saw the Martinez bunch come ridin' into town. I would suggest you leave as soon as possible."

"I'll be on the morning train to the capital. I still have to see Shorty before I can put this nasty business behind me."

Brady looked at him as if trying to decide what to do with him. "I reckon you wouldn't be safe ridin' out of here tonight anyway. You better sleep in the back of the jail. I'm sure it's not as grand as you're used to, but at least you won't be in any danger. I can't spare a man to play nursemaid to you all night. I've had to put extra men on just to keep things in hand as it is," he said indicating the deputies who still stood quietly behind him.

The next morning, Chad awoke stiff and sore from trying to sleep on the hard jail cot, but at least the night had passed without anymore trouble. He ate breakfast in the company of the sheriff, who relaxed a little and talked about his job. Chad felt that he was a man who could have been a good friend if it wasn't for all the trouble. They found that they both wanted to see the territory become a state, and both felt that the lawman and the courts were the only way to make the area fit to live in. Brady escorted him to the train, and they parted more amiably than Chad would have believed possible the night before.

Later, he sat across from Shorty Johnson, who had a guard at his right elbow. "'Bout time ya got here," Shorty grumbled. "I's beginnin' t' think yore ol' man had forsook me. I should have knowed ol' H. J. never lets his hands down."

Chad didn't like this man calling his father his old man.

He knew Marty did it with love and respect; this man didn't. He found that he liked Shorty even less than he had remembered. Somehow, Shorty seemed permanently soiled, not with the dirt and sweat of honest labor, but with some evil that oozed out of him. Wondering again why his father should care about this man, he tried to keep the contempt out of his voice as he said, "I'm just here to see if we can find some basis for a defense for you. Tell me what you remember about the shooting."

"Hell, there ain't much t' tell. These stinkin' sheepmen started a fight, an' one of 'em got himself shot. If it weren't fer that sheep lovin' sheriff, that'd be all."

"Did the man you shot have a knife as Frank claimed?"

Shorty shrugged. "Damned if I know. What's the difference? They was makin' fools outa me and Frank. It don't set good with me t' get beat—especially by no damned, stinkin' Mex' of a sheepman."

"In other words," Chad replied as calmly as he could, "You admit that you shot an unarmed man in cold blood."

Shorty looked puzzled. "What the hell difference does it make? All I done was t' rid the West of a stinkin' foreigner. Ya don't hang a man fer killin' a coyote."

Chad suddenly felt that he couldn't stand the smell of this place or of this man another moment. He didn't know what he was going to tell his father, but he wasn't going near this man again for any reason.

As he abruptly started for the door, a suddenly frightened Shorty called after him, "Hey, wait a minute. Ain't ya gonna get me out of here like yore ol' man promised?"

Chad never even turned around. As the door closed behind him, he could hear Shorty cursing him. For just a moment, he felt a spark of pity for the man, because he was sure that Shorty Johnson really didn't know any better.

He caught the afternoon train back to Silver City; he wasn't very surprised to be met at the station by Brady, who had Beau saddled and ready to ride. "I figured you would be back today. Havin' had the displeasure of Shorty's company before, I doubted that you could stand it for more than a minute or two. I know you aren't goin' to like this, but I think for your health and my peace of mind, you best be leaving right away."

"I hadn't intended to stay any longer than necessary, but I would have liked something to eat. It'll be dark long before I can make it even to Marysville."

Brady handed him a small bundle. "This'll keep you goin'. You can give me the money for your livery bill; I'll see that it gets paid. If you insist on visitin' us again, for awhile, be sure and check in with me."

So Chad ate another cold meal on the trail. This time he didn't even dismount to eat; he didn't take his time either. As it was, he didn't get into Marysville until late. It was a rather quiet night; a few miners from west of town plus a few drifters and the likes were all that were keeping the saloons open. Most of the cowhands were busy with the spring roundup, and the town wouldn't see very much of them for awhile. He was bone weary from two days traveling and his restless night in the jail, so he decided to stay in town instead of making the long ride home. Among other things, he was in no condition to face his father. Since the dining room was closed, all he could manage to get to eat was some pie and coffee. He barely made it to his room before collapsing across his bed, not even bothering to take off his boots. The room was just a small cubicle partitioned off with walls of brown paper, that didn't keep out the noise from the other rooms, but he was so tired he didn't hear a sound.

He awoke later than usual the next morning, feeling rested but very hungry. He went to the washstand and poured some water from the pitcher into the bowl. He washed, combed his hair, and straightened his clothes as much as possible before making his way to the dining room. After a double order of flapjacks, eggs and steak, washed down with a pot of hot coffee, he began to feel really good again. Since he was in town, he decided to see Sam Farris. Even though he didn't need to know any more about Shorty Johnson, a young lawyer could profit from having a friend with a newspaper. Besides, Farris seemed to be a friend of a young lady, whom he intended to get to know better.

Sam Farris was a little taken back by the appearance of the young man standing across from his desk. He looked as if he had been sleeping in his clothes; he had a two-day growth of beard. As Sam's glance traveled across his face, Chad raised his hand and ran it along his chin. He laughed at how he must look and said pleasantly, "I guess I must make some picture. I should have visited the barber before I came to see you."

Sam laughed with him and indicated a chair. "Sorry I can't get up, but I seem to have injured my ribs. It's too painful to move more than I have to. Can I help you with something?"

"I heard about your encounter at Sally's. I came by to see you day before yesterday, but your boy said you were still recuperating at home. I told Miss Grant to give you my best wishes."

Sam looked again at Chad's disheveled appearance and laughed. "You must be Winslow's son. Your father should see you now."Thinking about the expression on H. J.'s face at the sight of his son roaming around town looking like a drunken bum, made them both smile, and each felt at ease in the company of the other. Sam Farris was by nature a friendly, outgoing man who enjoyed good company, and he instinctively felt that Chad would be good company in spite of his father.

"Miss Grant told me you came by on your way to Silver City. Judging by your appearance, I would say that you didn't fare so well. In fact, I didn't expect you back here until late tonight."

"I didn't receive a warm welcome, that's for sure. I was waylaid and almost hanged by vengeful sheepmen, spent the night on a hard jail cot in 'protective custody,' rode to and from the capital in a few hours, and then rode straight to Marysville, where I collapsed on a hotel bed. Now that you know why I look like this, I hope you don't intend to make a news story about my condition."

Sam smiled reassuringly at him. "I couldn't make much of a story of that little bit of information unless I filled in the details myself, and despite what H. J. thinks, I don't add anything to the facts as I know them. Miss Grant said you had some questions about Shorty Johnson. I'll be glad to tell what I know."

Chad frowned at the mention of Shorty's name. "I don't think you can tell me anything I don't know at this point. As far as I'm concerned that is a closed subject. He should be tried in the next couple of days, and I imagine that he will be hanged shortly afterward."

"Does that mean that you will not be defending him?"

"I won't defend him. The court will have to appoint him a lawyer if he is to have one. He admits he killed the man, and I want no part of the case."

Sam started to lean back in his chair, winced from the pain of moving and decided to stay in an upright position. "Do you mind if I quote you? People around here would like to know that someone in the Winslow camp knows a murderer when he sees one."

That annoyed Chad a little; then, he probably was the only one around the ranch who thought Shorty was getting what he deserved. So, he ignored the statement and said, "I guess it won't matter. By the time you get the paper out, everyone at the ranch will know where I stand anyway." Both men thought of H. J. when he said that. Chad changed the subject by saying, "I was wondering about this Frank who started the fight in Sally's. Do you know anything about him?"

"Not much except he fancies himself a fighter—which is a joke. I understand he was with Shorty in Silver City."

"Yeah, apparently he had teamed up with Shorty, and they were on their way to hire on at our ranch. I figure my father would be doing himself a favor by getting rid of that man before he causes any more trouble."

"I doubt if he sees it that way though. I have just increased his loyalty to Frank by my article about him. You know your father doesn't think much of my paper."

"I got that idea from his reaction to your editorials," Chad laughed, remembering all the cursing it had caused.

As the young man walked out the door, Sam thought that he bore little resemblance to old man Winslow either in looks or manner. Now he understood why Melody's eyes had had that strange light in them when she had spoken of the young Winslow. He thought of Melody's unexplained hatred of the senior Winslow. Wouldn't that be something, if she fell for his son. Sam was soon at work on his copy about Chad's decision not to defend Shorty.

He knew it would be in the man's favor with many of the valley people, but it sure wouldn't be a popular stand around the Winslow ranch.

Since he needed a bath and a change of clothing, Chad decided it was useless to get a shave in town. So, he just rode on toward home, where he could really get himself cleaned up.

Rosie looked at him with obvious disapproval when he walked into the house. The ranch was practically deserted with all the men out rounding up cattle. Even his father was gone, for which Chad was grateful. He needed time to clean himself up and rest before the confrontation with his father.

Eight

"*Damn it, Marty.* What in tarnation's goin' on?" an enraged H. J. asked his foreman. "Who could be doin' this? Who would gain anythin' by it?"

Marty looked at the barbed wire hanging from the fence posts and shook his head. "Danged if I know. This here's the fourth section of wire the boys have found cut in the last two days. That's why I wanted you t' come have a look. I can't figure it out."

"Are we missin' many head?"

"Not any that I know of. It's mostly jest a nuisance. We have t' go lookin' fer the strayed cattle. Sometimes, they mix in with someone else's herd, an' we waste a lot of time cuttin' 'em out."

Winslow didn't like fooling around with the small operations, and the delay was an annoyance to him. "Don't you have any idea who is responsible?"

Marty got down from his horse and looked more closely at the ground. The cattle that had strayed through the hole in the fence had effectively masked any other prints which might have given them some clues. Standing up and looking off in the distance as if the answer would appear, he said, "No, I don't. The cuts are so scattered that it couldn't be one landowner with all the spreads that border our place. 'Sides, we ain't found any sign of brand changin'. Rustlin' don't seem t' be the motive."

"Are you dead sure about that, Marty? You don't think some of the new men could be coverin' up something? I'm sure about the regulars, but you never know about some of these drifters. Maybe they're in cahoots with one of the small outfits around here."

Marty shook his head. "Yes, I'm sure. I found this cut myself, an' some of the boys an' I went over t' see Thompson, who gave us his okay to round up our beeves. I bet he didn't even know they were on his land. They probably had only been there two or three days. Everything was in order. The young calves were still with their mothers an' still unbranded. There was even a couple of mavericks that he said must be ours because his herd wasn't that large. After all, if he had wanted to cheat us, he could have easily claimed those head as his. I let him keep one t' make up fer the trouble t' him."

"You're pretty damn generous with my cattle. Especially since I don't trust these people much. They all seem bent on takin' over around here."

Ignoring the remark about giving away his cattle, Marty just said, "I know how you feel, but you have t' trust me. You know I've seen enough changed brands an' freshly branded cattle t' know when I'm bein' lied to."

"If not rustlers, then who and why?"

"I can't tell you. Must be some kind of prank. After all, aside from costin' us some trouble an' time, it ain't gonna hurt us much. The cuttin' has all been in an area I figure is only a few hours ride from town. I would expect whoever cut these fences won't be able t' go much further. In any case, I have the men keepin' a close eye out fer any strangers 'round our land."

"You better be gettin' this fence fixed right away, before we lose some cows permanently."

"The cattle in this section have already been moved out. We got the last this mornin' an' I need all the men I have fer roundup an' brandin'. I was thinkin' Chad might like t' come out an' help me put up some fence. I'm gettin' a mite old fer all that rough stuff, an' he's still too green t' be much use. We're the only two what can be spared right now."

Winslow frowned and said with a touch of annoyance, "I'm not too crazy about my son stringin' barbed wire, but you can ask him. He seems to have a mind of his own now."

Marty ignored the tone of voice and said good naturedly, "Speakin' of Chad, you better get goin' if you want t' be at the ranch 'fore supper. There's a chance that he might be back by then." Getting back on his horse, he continued, "I'll likely be 'round the ol' Matthews place fer the next day or two. Tell Chad t' come on over an' see some real cowhands at work. Maybe he'll learn something."

"I don't want that boy breakin' his fool neck playin' cowboy."

"I remember the time you would have been out there fixin' it up yoreself."

"That was all right for you an' me. We didn't know anything better."

With that comment, H. J. rode toward the ranch house, while Marty started off in the other direction to check on his hands.

When Winslow arrived at the ranch, he was glad to see

Beau in the barn. He gave his horse to Ed, who cared for all Winslow's horses, and hurried into the house.

When he heard his dad come in, Chad was in the parlor, looking rested and considerably cleaner than before. He took a quick swallow of the drink he had been nursing and went to meet H. J. He had previously told Rosie to see to supper, and he would see that his father was comfortable and had a drink. She didn't need to get involved in what he expected to be a very unpleasant scene.

"Well, son, you got home sooner than I expected," H. J. said as soon as he was seated in his office where Chad had steered him, knowing it was the one room that Rosie wouldn't come into. "Tell me, how did it go? You look as though you had a restful trip."

"Actually, I've been home quite awhile. I didn't look like this when I rode in, but that is getting ahead of my story. You're not going to like what I have to tell you. So I want you to just listen to everything I have to say; then you can comment. Okay?"

The old man nodded. Chad told him about his meeting with Sheriff Brady which prompted H. J. to say, "I told you that sheriff was an idiot."

"I don't think so. If you will just listen until I'm through, you just might change your opinion of him."

"Okay, son. I doubt if you can say anything that will change my mind about him, but I won't interrupt you again."

Chad told him everything that had happened to him up until his night in jail before his father interrupted him again. "I have t' admit Brady showed some sense that time and probably did save your life. I guess I should be grateful, but I find it hard t' understand why he just let those Mexicans go. You can't trust any of 'em, anyhow."

"Those men were just grieving about what happened to their brother. They're not going to get into any more trouble."

"What were you doin' goin' t' see some priest for, in the first place? It looks like you were gettin' evidence t' hang Shorty instead of findin' a way t' free him."

"Dad, it is a lawyer's business to know as much about his case as possible. If I decided to defend him, I wanted to know what the prosecution would say. Anyway, you are missing the point entirely. Everyone in that town seems to think Shorty is guilty—even the cowmen."

H. J. was beginning to get a little red in the face as he asked, "Did you ever go see Shorty an' get his side of it? He doesn't think he's guilty, does he?"

"As a matter of fact, Shorty admitted to me that he shot the man. His only defense is that one sheepherder more or less doesn't matter much."

The old man shouted, "That's what I've been tryin' t' tell you. No one cares about sheepherders, anyway."

"I'm sure his wife, brothers and five children cared. A human life is always important, and no one can go around killing people just because their nationality or way of making a living offends him."

Seeing that his father was about to explode, Chad walked over to him and put his hands on H. J.'s shoulders. "I'm sorry if you are disappointed in me, but I just couldn't defend Shorty knowing he killed that man in cold blood. He is going to hang—with or without me. Don't let this no-account spoil things between us. We have a lot of time to make up for. Let's not start off mad at each other."

H. J. began to calm down and reached up, putting his hand over his son's. He said, "All right son, I don't understand your attitude, but I'll admit that you mean a powerful lot more t' me than Shorty.

"Rosie ought to have supper ready by now. Let's get a bit t' eat."

As they were walking to the dining room, H. J. muttered to himself, "I probably can find a lawyer in Silver City who will know a way to get Shorty off."

They did very little talking during supper. Chad was irritated that his dad was still concerned about Shorty's defense after he told H. J. that Shorty was guilty. H. J. was deep in thought about ways to get Shorty out of jail.

It wasn't until later that evening that H. J. remembered the fence cutting and told Chad all he knew about it. Chad wanted to ride out and look it over, but H. J. didn't want him around the men during the branding. He knew that they liked to fool around and put each other up to taking risks. Since Chad was a greenhorn, more or less, he would be the main target for their kidding. H. J. had seen men hurt trying to do something they weren't trained to do, and he didn't plan on letting it happen to his only son. He hadn't worked all these years to build up an empire just to see it go to some other family. Not telling Chad how he felt, for fear that Chad would be determined to prove him wrong, H. J. kept him busy going over some land claims and debt litigations. Chad figured he had angered his father enough, so he went along with what his father asked him to do. Over the next few days, the two men talked very little about anything but business since it seemed to be the only safe subject.

Nine

While Chad was busy humoring his father, Melody was sitting in her room feeling restless and frustrated because she wasn't accomplishing anything. Even though the school term would be over soon, she still didn't know what she was going to do during the recess. She needed a reason to stay in town during that time. More than that, she needed to see that she was doing some good here. It hadn't taken her long to realize that cutting Winslow's fences was only a minor annoyance to him. The only way it would cause him any real trouble was if she could rustle some of his cattle, but she didn't have any place to take them or any way to change the brands. Enlisting the aide of some local small rancher would take care of that problem, but she didn't want to encourage someone else to steal. Besides, this was her own personal vendetta which she meant to carry out alone. Even Sam and Lenore didn't know where she had gone on her evening rides.

She had only been able to cut a few sections of fence anyway, because the Winslow spread was so large. By the time school was out every afternoon, she didn't have enough time to ride to more than just a small portion of his land. Cutting what she would be able to get to in the first two nights, she had realized that she couldn't make it much farther and get back to town at a decent hour. In fact, on Tuesday night, she had ridden farther than she realized and hadn't gotten back to the livery stable until very late. Surprised to see the hostler wiping down Chad Winslow's beautiful roan, she was told that she had just missed him. Melody had felt her heart give a little jump which was not entirely due to the questions he would have asked if he had seen her out so late at night. Admittedly, she had been hoping to see him the next day; she didn't. Sam had told them at the supper table that night about Chad's visit to the paper.

It pleased her that Sam thought well of Chad, but Chad or no Chad, she had to find a way to get even with H. J. What she needed now was an excuse to get close to the main house. She had seen the Winslow hands rounding up cattle and figured they would be away from the main house for a while, since she had heard that they would be doing their branding around the old Matthews corrals.

The slam of the back door and Sam's cheery call to his wife interrupted her thoughts so she went downstairs into the kitchen to see if Lenore needed any help putting supper on. As they ate, Sam told them all the news of the day. It all passed her by until she heard H. J.'s name.

Sam was saying, "Winslow won't be very happy about this. I feel a little sorry for Chad when he gets the news."

Melody asked, "When he gets what news?"

Sam and Lenore both looked at her oddly before Sam answered, "I just told you. Shorty Johnson was hanged this morning. They sure don't fool around much once they convict them. His trial was only yesterday."

"Do you think H. J. knows?"

"I doubt it. I have the quickest source to the capital, and I've only known about an hour. I'm going back to finish setting the story after we eat."

An idea was forming in Melody's head, and she muttered, more to herself than anyone else, "I suppose Chad would like to know."

"I reckon he would at that. If I wasn't still so sore, and if I didn't think that H. J. might shoot me on sight, I would ride out and tell him. With the roundup on, it could be days before they get into town for a paper."

"Listen, Sam, tomorrow is Saturday; since there is no school, I could ride out and tell Mr. Winslow. I'm sure even H. J. wouldn't shoot a lady on sight. Frankly, I've been frightfully curious about that house. I've heard it is the prettiest in the whole territory."

"Oh, haven't we all! Everytime I get together with the other ladies in town, the talk eventually turns to the Winslow house. Madge Baker has been in the front entry once. She went out there with her husband, and H. J. never asked them in where she could see anything." Lenore sighed. "I would like to be the first one to see that place."

"Lenore, I have a great idea. Why don't you come with me? It will look a lot better for two ladies to ride out there than one. I'll bet Chad Winslow wouldn't leave two ladies outside when they came to give him some important news."

Sam laughed. "Can you beat that? Here's a girl who rides around the country in men's clothes, refusing to sit sidesaddle like a proper lady, and she's worried about how it looks for her to come up to a man's house alone."

"All right, Sam," chided Lenore. "She's right. Besides, I haven't been away from the house in such a long time. I'll bet we could use Mrs. Perry's buggy. She rarely uses it any more, and she is such a lovely person. If you have to be at the paper, I could get Betty Lou to watch the children for me."

Sam smiled and patted his wife's hand fondly. "I don't mind you going. I realize you work hard around here, and I can see the look of anguish on Mrs. Baker's haughty face when she finds out that you actually saw the inside of that house."

"Then it's all settled." Melody smiled to herself, causing the Farrises to exchange knowing looks. While they thought that her smile was in anticipation of seeing the young Mr. Winslow, she was actually picturing how she could sweet-talk him into giving her a tour of the outbuildings on the ranch. She had very little interest in the main house. This just might work out nicely.

The next day was a beautiful one, bursting with the colors and sounds of spring, and the women enjoyed their ride in the open buggy. Melody had chosen her outfit very carefully and had spent a long time arranging her hair flawlessly under her new hat, because she had every intention of charming the wits out of both the Winslows. Having had plenty of practice in proper female persuasion in St. Louis, she intended to put it to good use.

Chad was outside, practicing with his gun, when he first saw the buggy approaching. At that distance, he couldn't tell who was in it, but he saw the feathered hats and parasols soon enough to inform Rosie that they were about to have female company. By the time the buggy pulled up in front of the house, Chad had delightedly realized who was driving.

Lenore had to work hard to keep from laughing at the sheepish look on Chad's face as he offered Melody his hand. As the genteel-looking lady stepped daintily from the carriage, an image of her with her hair flying behind her as she jumped her horse over a fence popped into his head. There was much about this woman that was a mystery to him.

"Good day, ladies. I hope you didn't come all the way out here to see my father. He rode out this morning to check on the men, and I'm afraid he won't be home until very late, if at all."

As he helped Mrs. Farris to the ground, Melody said, "No, Mr. Winslow, we actually came to see you. This is Lenore Farris; her husband asked us to deliver a message to you. It's probably just as well that your father isn't here, for I fear he will not be pleased with our news."

Chad took the hand that Lenore offered him and said, politely, "I'm very happy to meet you, Mrs. Farris. I do hope that your husband has recovered."

Lenore answered, "He is doing better every day, but he is still not up to such a long ride."

Chad called Ed and told him to take the horses and buggy around back. Then, taking each woman by the elbow, he led them toward the house. "Well, Miss Grant, what is this news you bring me?"

"Mr. Farris felt that you would want to know that Mr. Johnson was hanged yesterday morning."

Even though he had figured that was what they were here for, Chad stopped abruptly at Melody's words. He felt a sense of relief that it was over, which was quickly followed by the awareness of what his father would have to say about this. He frowned slightly as he said, "I appreciate you coming to tell me. It will probably be awhile before anyone around here gets a chance to go into Marysville to get a paper."

"Oh, dear. Speaking of the paper, I have one in the buggy, but I forgot to give it to you," Melody said.

"Thank you, I'll get it when you are ready to leave."

Lenore said, "You don't seem surprised to hear that he was hanged, Mr. Winslow."

"No, I expected it. I just wasn't sure when."

"Will your father be upset?" Melody inquired.

Chad noticed that she wasn't having so much trouble talking about his father as usual. Maybe he had imagined the edge in her voice before. Anyway, with her standing so close to him, he didn't really want to discuss his father. "I'll just say that he isn't going to feel as I do about it." He started walking again with a lady on either side of him. "We better get you out of this sun. I believe our house-keeper has some tea and cakes or something ready. She loves to show off her skills, but we so seldom have any ladies to visit."

The three of them went into the parlor where Rosie had indeed set up a very impressive tray of sweets and fancy sandwiches to eat with their tea. Melody hadn't seen such an elegant room since she left St. Louis. Lenore had only dreamed of such luxury: the gleam of highly polished woods, the warmth of thick velvet draperies, the intricate detail of rich brocades, and, most fascinating of all to her, the delicate grace of the expensive china figures. It was very hard not to stare.

Melody was enchanted by an elaborately carved up-right grand piano. "Oh, it is beautiful. It has been so long since I have played. I think that is what I miss most out here—good music," she exclaimed, as she ran her hands almost reverently over the keys.

"It hasn't been played in a long time, but I would love to have you play for us, if you would. I used to love to hear my mother play."

Melody hesitated just a moment before she sat down and began to play a Beethoven sonata with skill and great feeling. One thing she was grateful for in St. Louis was the chance to learn the piano. Both Chad and Lenore were surprised and impressed by her performance. Afterwards, they had their tea and talked about town gossip. They all complimented a beaming Rosie on her food. Then, the two women were offered the chance to freshen up before their return trip.

As they stepped out the front door, Melody saw that Chad had already had their buggy brought around. She turned to him and said sweetly, "Mr. Winslow, I've never seen a real ranch like this before. Would you be so kind as to show me around a bit before we go?"

"Of course. I would be glad to show you around, but would you please call me Chad?"

Lenore begged off the tour, saying she wanted to get a recipe from Rosie. The two young people walked off together. Lenore and Rosie beamed at the couple from inside the house as they toured the other buildings that made up the main ranch complex. They were both laughing and smiling, and even from a distance, it was easy to see that they were enjoying each other's company. Flattering Chad by her close attention to everything he said, Melody catalogued in her mind the locations and uses of the outbuildings on the ranch. Chad introduced her to Ed and Bob, who cared for the horses. Very impressed by the conformation of the blooded ranch horses, Melody showed a great deal of knowledge about them. Even with Chad adding as much detail as possible, it still didn't take them long to make their way back to the house; soon, the two women were driving off.

On the way back to town, Lenore raved about how lovely the house was and how nice it must be to have that kind of money. She was also quite excited about being the first in her circle of friends to have actually seen the inside of the house. She figured now that the younger Winslow was home there would be more people visiting the ranch, since he was such a likable young man.

As Lenore chattered on about all this, Melody was busy fighting an inner battle. She was beginning to like Chad Winslow more and more, and she wasn't sure how that would fit in with her plans to get even with his father. If she did manage to hurt H. J., wouldn't she hurt Chad too? Well, she only needed one more thing from him. She needed to know where Basin River branched. In dry weather, H. J. would close off the gate in a dam he had built on the secondary branch, leaving many of the other places without water since the main stream ran almost entirely through his land. More than one small rancher or farmer had had to pull out because of this; she intended to do something about it if it happened again. If she could get Chad to take her to the dam, then she wouldn't have to see him again, and she could go back to thinking about her fiancé. After all, before the year was up, she hoped to be back in St. Louis and married.

That night and all day Sunday, she carefully planned her next move. This time she waited until it was dark, because she didn't want anyone to see her leave town. Sneaking out of the house after the Farrises were all asleep, she managed to get Fortune without encountering the hostler. Over her usual outfit, she wore a fringed buckskin jacket, and she had carefully braided her hair, winding it around her head so her hat pretty much covered it. If by chance she was spotted, she hoped to be taken for a man. By the time she got to the Winslow spread, it was very late. Just as she had hoped everybody appeared to be asleep. She figured H. J., Chad, and Rosie would be in the house. The two men she had met yesterday would be sleeping in the bunkhouse, and she didn't plan on bothering it. There were only a few horses around now; they were all in the barn for the night. Her only worry was whether her presence in the area would start them whinnying.

Leaving Fortune in a grove of trees several yards from the buildings, she silently crawled across the open area to the back door of the carriage house. As she carefully opened the door, the collection of buckboards, buggies, and an elegant surrey seemed to mock her. Her mind flashed back to a long-ago day when she and her mother had seen Mrs. Winslow out riding in that surrey. Mrs. Winslow had been very rude to her mother; ever since, Melody had hated the sight of a surrey carrying a proud lady.

The moonlight shining through the cracks in the boards lit up the place enough for her to see what she was doing. She made her way to the front of the building where she had seen a kerosene lantern hanging on a hook. Taking it down, she unscrewed the cap and spread the kerosene over the loose hay lying around. She found another lantern and spread its kerosene over the seats in some of the rigs. Then she took a match from her jacket pocket, struck it on a wagon wheel hub and threw it into the soggy mess. One quick flash and there was fire everywhere. Dashing out the back door, she ran all the way to the trees where she could see what was happening without being seen.

When she had looked the place over yesterday, she

had calculated that she could safely burn the carriage house without endangering any of the people or horses. She didn't want to kill anything—just give Winslow a little taste of his own medicine, since she knew that burning out sheepherders had been his standard method of dealing with that menace.

As soon as they got a sniff of smoke, the horses began to nicker and stamp around; soon, she saw lamps go on in the house and the bunkhouse. Mr. Winslow came running out of the house closely followed by Chad and Rosie. She wasn't close enough to see their faces, but she could identify them by their sizes; H. J. was several inches shorter and many pounds heavier than his son, while Rosie was very short and very heavy. The two men from the bunkhouse reached the fire first and headed straight for the barn.

Sitting back feeling very pleased with herself, Melody suddenly realized with a shock that some of the burning debris had blown onto the barn roof next to the carriage house, and the barn was going to go up very fast. She had been so sure that they were far enough apart to prevent that from happening. Her heart began beating loudly, and she broke out in a cold sweat. Dear God, she prayed, don't let those beautiful animals die. For a moment, she almost considered riding down and helping them get the horses out, but she knew that she could only watch in horror while the five people worked frantically to save the horses.

By now, the sky was lit up as the angry flames raced through the two buildings. H. J. started for the carriage house, but Chad pushed him toward the barn, shouting something that was lost in the night wind. One of the men came out of the barn leading a horse with some kind of cloth over its head. He was having a lot of trouble because the animal was trying to get away from him and turn back into the fire. Dodging the flying sparks and falling timbers, Chad and H. J. made their way into the barn, soon reappearing with a horse each.

Even Rosie went into the burning barn. As she came back out, leading a beautiful white horse, Melody noticed that Rosie's long robe was burning around the hem. She thought it was Chad who grabbed Rosie and threw her down in the dirt, rolling her around until the flames were out. Apparently Rosie was all right because she got up right away. After that she didn't go into the barn again, but she would take the horses from the men as they came out of the barn, and lead them into a corral out of danger.

Soon the horses were all safe, and the weary figures just stood helplessly and watched the two buildings burn. It was a good thing that all the other buildings were far enough away to avoid the same fate. Too weak and frightened to move, Melody just sat there almost until dawn, watching the havoc she had created. Finally, she rode off in just enough darkness to cover her going. There was a bitter taste in her mouth in sharp contrast to the sweet taste of victory that she had anticipated.

Ten

Chad rummaged half-heartedly through the debris, occasionally finding a hot spot. His hand blistered where he had put out the fire on Rosie's robe, he was bone weary and covered with black soot. He had sent Rosie back to bed after they had the horses safe, but the rest of them were still outside. Since there wasn't any feed left in the barn, he sent the two men to move the horses out to pasture. Then he went over to where his father stood dejectedly looking at the pile of rubbish that had once carried a proud and beautiful lady.

H. J. turned to him with a stricken face as Chad came close. "Who could have done this? Who?"

Chad replied with surprise plain in his voice, "Do you really think someone actually set this on purpose? Fires do happen."

H. J.'s face grew dark with hatred as he answered, "Someone set it, I tell you! Someone's out to get me! I know it! I just know it!"

His reply was so venomous that Chad didn't argue with him. Chad's relationship with his father had deteriorated a great deal since he had told H. J. about Shorty's hanging. Now was not the time for him to disagree with H. J. about anything, so he just said, "Well, I'll check around. If anyone was here there should be some sign."

Before they could do anything else, they heard Rosie ringing the dinner bell. They hadn't even thought of breakfast, but now they both realized that it was getting pretty late in the morning. Since the cowhands' cook was out with the men, Rosie had been taking some grub to the two men in the bunkhouse. This time Chad told her to feed them in the kitchen of the house, figuring the bunkhouse and cookshack probably smelled of smoke.

It was a silent meal; the only sounds were the rattling of utensils and the slurping noise the hands made drinking their coffee. H. J. and Chad had elected to eat in the kitchen too, since they were so dirty. Chad was trying to figure out what made his father so sure that the fire had been set, and H. J. was thinking of what he would do when he found out who had dared to destroy his property. The two others were very uncomfortable about being in the big house, especially eating at the same table with the boss; they were too new to remember when H. J. had taken all his meals with the hands.

After eating and before bathing, Chad went out to the still smoldering pile of rubbish that had once been a carriage house filled with expensive rigs. Near what had been the back door he found part of a lantern, which surprised him because no one ever used that door. Examining the ground, he found a set of footprints leading away into the grove of trees to the north. Momentarily puzzled by the single set of prints, he wondered why there were no tracks leading into the building. It didn't take a great tracker to know a man had to come in before he could go out. Then he discovered what looked like a small handprint in the dirt. Then another one.

"That's how he did it," he said out loud. "He must have crawled in and run out. It looks like the old man was right after all."

"Of course, I'm right." His father's voice made him start. Crouched on his hands and knees, Chad hadn't seen him come up. The old man went on, "I've seen enough fires in my time t' know when one's been set on purpose."

"If no one set the fire, there was still someone fooling around here who shouldn't have been. I'm going to follow the footprints and see where they go. Probably into those trees."

H. J. swore. "The low-down skunk must have sat up there in the trees an' watched everything."

Chad followed the prints right into the grove of trees, finding the spot where a horse had been tied and where someone had sat in the bushes. Since they hadn't seen anyone leave this morning, he felt sure that whoever it was had been gone a long time. There was no use in trying to follow him now. If he had any sense, he would have gone into the river a mile down the road, and Chad knew he would lose the trail there.

He walked back to where his father stood. "You're right about the trees. From the manure and freshly pawed up ground, I would say a horse had been there for quite awhile. I never realized before how much you can see from there."

"I never knew that you can't see a man when he gets int' those trees. You disappeared several times while you were walkin' 'round up there."

"Maybe you ought to have them thinned out some."

H. J. spoke so low that Chad could barely make out

what he was saying. "That won't be necessary. From now on, I intend t' have men on guard all the time 'round here. First my fences—now, my buildin's. Someone is out t' get me, an' they won't stop there!"

After a long soak in some very hot water, Chad put on clean clothes and was just settling down for a short nap when his father pounded on the door. Startled at the loud noise, Chad jumped up. In his half-asleep state, the sound had hurled him back to last night when his father had shouted at him to get up. He had opened his eyes to see the flames from the carriage house dancing on his ceiling; it had taken him a minute to realize the fire was outside.

This time his father just wanted to talk to him. Chad propped himself up against his brass bed and listened as his father paced the floor, ranting and raving about all the nesters, sheepherders, and other outsiders who were trying to take everything away from him. Nearly every other word was a curse word making it difficult to understand him.

"I'm goin' int' town first thing tomorrow an' see that Farris. He's always so blamed anxious t' print something bad about me. Let's see him print something bad about the other side for once. I want you t' ride out an' find Marty. He should be at the Matthews place yet. Tell him what happened an' that I want a couple of men back here t' keep an eye on things until I can make other arrangements."

Chad knew how things would turn out if his father went into town in the mood he was in. Besides, Chad had a few questions he wanted answered, and Sam was probably the man to do it. He said, "Dad, why don't I go see Sam? You should talk to Marty yourself. You know the men, and you might want to pick who you feel you can trust."

H. J. thought for a minute. Chad probably figured he would lose his temper with Sam. Well, maybe he was right. Chad had a better way with people than he did. "Okay, son, but you tell Sam Farris that I want him t' put in his article about what's been happenin' 'round here, that anyone who steps on my land from now on will be shot."

Chad frowned as he said, "You know that I can't tell Sam what to print. He's pretty independent."

"If he doesn't want t' write it up in the article, you take out an ad. In fact, that might be better, anyway. Buy a full page ad that says from now on the Winslows shoot first an' ask questions later."

Chad felt a sense of impending doom as his father spoke.

Early the next morning, the two men rode off in different directions. Chad tried to follow the trail he had seen yesterday, but just as he had figured the rider had entered the river, making it impossible to pick up the trail again. Marty was the only one Chad knew who was able to track that well. The education he could have gotten from Marty would probably have stood him in better stead in this country than his college degree. Giving up on trying to follow the mysterious rider, he rode on into town, heading straight for the newspaper office.

Sam was surprised but seemed pleased to see him. He listened without comment while Chad told him about the strange goings-on at the Winslow spread. When Chad had finished, Sam asked, "You think it was a boy?"

"If it wasn't, it was a mighty small man. Even the hand prints were much smaller than mine."

"I've been afraid of something like this for quite awhile now."

Chad asked with surprise, "What? You have some idea who is responsible?"

"No, Chad, I didn't say that. It's hard to say this to you, but there's a lot of bad blood between the small outfits around here and your father. There are many people who would feel justified in doing any or all of these things. You said that no cattle had disappeared, which rules out rustlers, and whoever burned the carriage house and barn could have burned the main house if he got that close. I would say someone is trying to get back at your father but doesn't want to really hurt anyone. Could be a young man who feels his family is being hurt by something your father did. Still, your father may be wise to be on his guard."

"He's way ahead of you, Sam," Chad said as he pulled a paper out of his coat pocket and handed it to him. "He wants to take out this ad—full page, no less. I know it is a bit much, but you know how he is."

Sam read the paper and put it down, saying, "Maybe it is a good idea. I'll be willing to print it. It might just keep someone from getting himself killed."

"You said there is bad blood between my father and some of the people around here. Would you be willing to tell me what you meant by that? I know that he has always considered this valley his, but that's no reason to burn a man's property down."

Sam looked rather doubtful about what he was going to say, but after several attempts at clearing his throat, he finally started. "Chad, I have felt from the first time I met you that you were a man I would like to know better. I sure hate to spoil what could be a good friendship before it really has a chance. Maybe you should ask someone else about that."

"Part of being a man's friend should be the willingness to tell him the truth. Besides, you know that I don't know anybody around here except the people at the ranch—with the exception of you and Miss Grant." Chad stopped as if remembering something. He continued, "That is another thing that puzzles me. She almost spits out my father's name as if she hated him. Yet, neither he nor Marty Simpson even seem to know her. How could she hate someone she doesn't even know—or could I be imagining it?"

"No, I've noticed it too, but I honestly don't know what the problem could be. As far as I know, she never set foot in this valley until recently."

Chad leaned over the desk and looked Sam straight in the eye. "Sam, I need to know what is going on. I'm asking you to tell me, because I don't think you would lie to me. Many times my mother wrote me about things that didn't make sense to me. Someday, I will own that ranch and half of this town that bares my mother's name. I need to know what has been going on around here while I was away growing up."

"All right, Chad. I guess you have as much right as anyone to know everything I know. You know that I've only been here a little over two years; so I don't have any first-hand knowledge about anything that happened before that. I think everything you want to know is in the old papers in the back room. You're sure welcome to look through them, and I'll answer any questions that you have about what you find there. All I can say is that I have always tried to be as accurate as possible and not to be biased for or against anyone."

Chad spent the next few hours searching through most of the papers Sam had published. Since the paper had only been printed once a week at first, there wasn't too much news of any interest for the first six months. After awhile, he found a lot of articles concerning his father, especially as the area began to grow. From a legal standpoint, there was very little hard evidence of any wrong doing on H. J.'s part. Still, it wasn't hard to see how people could feel bitter toward him. It seemed that the Winslow cowhands had a reputation for beating up anyone who got in their way—especially nesters or sheepmen. Several sheepherders had been burned out by a bunch who were said to be Winslow's men. Then, there was the business of the dam across Basin River. Sam claimed that was why Matthews had to leave the valley. When he couldn't get the water for his crops and livestock, Matthews had been forced to sell to H. J., who was the only one in the valley with any money that year. Sam made it very clear that he considered that Matthews had been taken.

Finally, Chad couldn't take any more and came out of the back, shouting at Sam, "If these are accurate, it looks like half the territory has a reason to burn my father out!" He would have said more, but he was shaken by the sight of Melody Grant. He was so engrossed with how lovely she looked, that he didn't even notice Mrs. Farris at first.

Melody winced at the sight of his bandaged hand. She was horrified to find herself face to face with him so soon after the fire. Staring at his hand, she was reminded of how close she came to really injuring someone.

Lenore spoke first. "Good afternoon, Mr. Winslow. It's so nice to see you again. When we decided to drop in on my husband, we didn't have any idea that you would be here."

Chad was having trouble keeping his eyes off Melody.

He continued to look at her, but tipped his hat to Mrs. Farris. He said, "Good afternoon, ma'am."

"Are you going to be in town at suppertime? If so, we would love to have you eat with us."

"Thank you, but I'll have to wait on that invitation. I have to be going." Chad turned to Sam and said, "I have to see my father about a few things."

Chad started for the door, but Lenore called after him. "Did my husband mention the social at the schoolhouse this Friday night? We are hoping to get some more people interested in helping us finish the church building. We would love to have you go with us. You could escort Miss Grant. I've heard that your mother was a God-fearing woman, and I'm sure that she would have loved for there to be a church in these parts."

"Yes, Mrs. Farris, I'm sure she would have. If I'm able to be in town that night I would be glad to escort Miss Grant." Turning to Melody, he asked, "It is all right with you?"

Stunned by the turn of events, Melody just nodded.

"Well, then," Lenore said, "It's all settled. We'll expect you around seven."

Eleven

Chad rode out of town with his head swimming. In one afternoon it seemed his life had taken two rather unexpected turns. First, he had read some things which raised serious questions about his father. Second, he was going to a social with the prettiest girl he had ever met—a pretty girl who seemed to have something against his father. He had never thought of his father as a saint, but he had never imagined him as Sam Farris painted him either. Yet, in spite of himself, he felt sure that Sam was an honest man. Needing to talk to someone who could help him sort the whole thing out, he rode toward the branding corrals, hoping to find Marty and not H. J. Since he had been a little kid, the one person he could always go to for straight answers had been Marty.

It was suppertime before he made it to where the boys and Marty were, and he was relieved to find that his father wasn't around. Knowing that he wouldn't be able to talk to Marty privately for awhile, Chad accepted the beans, bacon and biscuits he was offered. He hadn't eaten since breakfast, which made the simple fare taste even better than usual. He liked being with Marty and the men; he began to relax some as they sat around the fire swapping stories while someone strummed a guitar accompanied by a so-so harmonica. This was one of the little luxuries that the men had been denied in the days of the long drives. Here, with the cattle all packed safely in a corral, there was little danger of them being spooked and stampeding.

Marty carefully rolled himself a cigarette and said quietly to Chad, "The ol' man didn't say anythin' 'bout you showin' up. Somethin' happen in town?"

Chad took another drink of coffee and then answered, "I'll tell you about it later. Did the old man go back to the ranch?"

"Nope, he said he had some business t' take care of an' would be gone fer a spell. It's unusual fer him t' not tell me where he was goin' or why."

Chad felt uneasy about his father riding off like that, but he didn't say that to Marty. However, Marty sensed his uneasiness and changed the subject. "If you're plannin' on hangin' 'round a bit, I'd like t' get those fences restrung. Did H. J. tell you that I needed yore help?"

"No, he didn't mention anything to me about fixing any fences."

Marty nodded his head in understanding. "I think it galled him some I was askin' his son t' string wire like a hired hand, but I can't spare any of these men right now. Now that he sent two more men back t' the main house t' keep an eye on things, I'm even more shorthanded. In the old days, the ol' man would always work side by side with me, just like one of the hands. I didn't expect him t' be insulted by my idea."

"Don't worry about it, Marty. You know I would be glad to help. Before I will be helpful with the branding, I'll need more experience roping, among other things, but that'll have to wait. Right now, I need to talk to you alone. Stringing wire will give us a chance to talk and get some work done, too." Deciding to leave the conversation there, he asked, "Where's Frank? I haven't seen him, and I was wondering how he took the news about Shorty."

"Yore ol' man sent him back t' the main house t' help guard the place. I don't know why, but anyway, it gets him away from here. He has been the brunt of a lot of jokes over his fight with Farris, an' I'm pretty sick of foolin' with him."

"I think you would be saving yourself a lot of trouble, if you just fired him."

Marty took a long drag off his cigarette before he asked, "What did yore ol' man say 'bout firin' him?"

Chad frowned as he remembered that conversation. "He said Frank stays."

"Then he stays."

Chad started to say more, but one of the men came over and sat down close to them, changing the talk to how the work was going. Any other time Chad would have enjoyed listening to the men talk about their work and compare things with the old days of the long drives to Abilene. There was a lot of good-natured kidding about different men's skills or lack of them, and he knew that, although this was hard work, it was work the men looked forward to. Some of these men had spent lonely months in line shacks and were happy to be with their own kind again. Knowing they had a long, hard day ahead of them, the men soon sacked out. Chad borrowed a blanket and found a spot to lie down. It wasn't the hard ground that kept him awake. It was the questions that Sam had raised in his mind, and even more, the memory of those clear blue eyes looking so pained at the sight of him.

For a while the next morning, Chad watched the men at work. Marty was cutting out the calves for branding, and watching him work had always fascinated Chad. Marty and his horse worked together as if they were one. Just the slightest bit of pressure from Marty's leg and the horse knew just which animal to separate from the others. He always said that cutting out calves took know-how, a good eye, and a top notch horse; he had all three. Soon the cow and calf were cut out, and a man heel-roped the calf and dragged the bawling animal toward the long fire pit where the branding irons were heated. Then one man grabbed the calf's head and another the tail end; flipping him over, they held him down by stretching him out. The brander pressed the iron hard on the flank of the unhappy critter. While it was down, another man with a sharp knife, quickly made it a steer, and then the animal was released to return to its mother.

After awhile, one of the men drove up in a buckboard with two spools of wire, and after Chad had loaded enough supplies to last him and Marty a couple of days, the two men rode off toward the cut sections of fence. Chad was glad to finally have Marty to himself, but he really didn't know where to begin the conversation. Marty broke the silence. "Okay, son, tell me what's eatin' ya. You've been actin' like yore britches was on fire ever since you rode in here last night."

"Frankly, Marty, I don't know where to start. So much has happened since I last saw you."

"Start with Shorty, an' yore trip t' Silver City. Yore ol' man came in here yesterday in a powerful hurry, muttered something 'bout you, an' Shorty's hanging, an' a fire, told me t' send two men t' the ranch house t' keep an eye on things an' lit out. It didn't make much sense."

Chad told Marty all about his trip to Silver City and his talk with Shorty, which surprised Marty, who had heard a different version of the shooting from H. J. Then, Chad told him about his decision not to defend Shorty and about Shorty's hanging. He explained his father's idea that whoever had set the fire would be back to do more damage. Finally, he told him about his visit to Sam. "That's mainly what I've been so upset about. Sam said there were a lot of people who would think they had good reason to burn my father out."

"Yeah, I reckon there's a few."

"Marty, I've read everything Sam ever wrote about my father, and there is very little that would make a son proud. I never figured my father was a saint, but I sure didn't see him like that." Chad was talking so fast that Marty could hardly follow him, let alone get in a word of his own. "On top of that, I really was beginning to like Sam Farris, and I find it hard to believe that he is an out and out liar."

Marty urged the team on and then said slowly, "I never thought of Sam as a liar. He jest sees things different from cowmen. He's an Easterner come out here t' make a little money publishin' land claims an' the like, an' I figure he got a little taste of the power that comes with a paper, an' it went t' his head a bit. There ain't nothing noble 'bout printin' bad things 'bout the down and out. Somehow, it always seems like a good thing if you can say something bad 'bout the big guys."

"Come on, Marty, there has to be more to it than that. Remember, you're not talking to a kid. I know a little about the law, and Sam isn't fool enough to take a chance on printing something unless he is sure of the facts."

"Well, the facts he prints are true enough, I guess, but he draws some strange conclusions from 'em. What happened to the Matthewses, for example. One of the reasons yore father has controlled this valley so long is he controls the water. The main channel of the Basin River is mostly on his property. There is a secondary channel that flows through the western part of the valley, where Matthews and a family called Chaffin once tried t' settle. When it's a good, wet year, both of these channels run fairly high an' there's water fer everybody. In a dry year, there's barely enough fer our place. H. J. built a dam across the secondary branch that helps us control the water flow. He owns the dam, and the water. Two years back, we had a mild winter an' a dry spring, an' things looked bad. We needed all the water we could get, but when we closed the floodgate in the dam to give us more water, Sam said H. J. was pushin' Matthews out. There was hardly any water runnin' through there, anyway. When the expected happened an' Matthews went broke, there wasn't anyone 'round who could afford t' bail him out except yore ol' man. When he did, there were people who resented it."

Chad said with some annoyance, "He didn't do himself any harm. That's for sure. I remember he wanted that place for years."

"Yeah, but he didn't steal it. He gave 'em more than anyone else would have. Believe me, if we had of given 'em the water they wanted, we would have lost at least half of our herd. Yore father tried t' tell those people in the first place that there weren't enough water 'round here fer so many spreads—they wouldn't listen."

That day and the next, while they worked and ate together, Marty carefully explained away most of what

Chad had read in Sam's back issues. According to Marty, H. J. had been guilty only of looking out for himself and the future of his spread which he hoped would belong to Winslows for generations. H. J. didn't come out lily-white, but it was clear that there wasn't enough evidence to even try him with, let alone convict him. By the time they were through repairing fences, Chad was beginning to see the whole thing as a difference of viewpoint.

As the two men rode back toward the Matthews corrals, they came across the old Chaffin place where they had first seen Melody. Chad asked, "Did these people leave because of water problems, too?"

Marty was obviously more troubled about what had happened here than about the other things he had explained. He did feel that Chad should know, so he answered, "No, they must have left 'bout eight years back. That was a good year 'round here, an' there was plenty of water fer everyone. In fact, we didn't even put in the floodgate 'til the next year or so. Chaffin was a stubborn man, who insisted on puttin' his blamed farm right here in the middle of our usual trail. We have driven cattle through that pass yonder, an' this side of the valley, ever since we've been here. H. J. an' I tried more than once t' convince him that he could jest as easily farm a little t' the west, but he insisted the land wasn't as good. Anyway, on fall roundup that year, the boys decided not t' bother goin' 'round an' they jest pushed the cattle right through his place. They sure enough made a mess of the place, but they didn't mean to hurt no one."

At this point, Marty got a far-away look and was clearly disturbed by the memory. Chad started to tell him whatever had happened wasn't important, but Marty continued, staring straight ahead as he talked, as though he couldn't look at Chad's face. "I wasn't with the boys, yet—after all these years, I don't remember why—I was in the barn at the ranch when I heard a man shoutin' in front of the house. He was callin' H. J. a murderer, an' I stepped out of the barn jest in time t' see him shoot H. J. in the shoulder. Without taking time t' aim or even thinkin' 'bout what I was doin', I shot him twice. I had to, Chad, or he would have killed yore father, who wasn't even armed. It was Mr. Chaffin, who blamed yore ol' man because his son was killed by the stampeding cattle. After helpin' yore mother get H. J. inside, I slung Chaffin 'cross his horse an' took him home. He died a couple of days later. So, Mrs. Chaffin buried two men in less than a week an' then she left. Matthews took over their land, although I don't know how legal it was. Anyway, no one ever heard of Mrs. Chaffin, again."

"Didn't she have any other children?" Chad asked.

"There was a girl there when I took Chaffin home, but I don't know who she was."

"Mother wrote me that someone had shot dad, but she never said why. I remember thinking what an awful thing to do, but I guess he felt he had reason to be angry."

"Yeah, I suppose, but the fool jest wouldn't listen. Chad you have t' understand, I didn't have any choice. If I had taken the time at that distance t' try an' jest wound him, he could have killed yore father." He turned to look at Chad for the first time since he had started the story. He was wet with perspiration although the day was fairly cool. "Other than in the war, I ain't ever killed another man. The few times I've had t' draw my gun, I've been able t' settle things with nothing more than a shoulder wound or a shot-up hand. I jest couldn't help that." He shook his head as if to shake away a troublesome memory.

Chad couldn't think of anything to say. He really didn't understand why a right of way was so important, but he loved Marty and believed that he didn't like to kill anyone. Besides, it was pretty hard to blame a man for saving your father's life. In a way he was sorry he had brought the subject up, but it was good for him to know exactly what had happened in case it ever came up again. They rode in silence back to the corrals. For a couple of days Chad hung around watching the work, and occasionally lent a hand when he could. Then on Friday, he shook hands with Marty and headed back for the house to freshen up for his date.

Everything was pretty quiet around the place, except that Rosie was in a snit about having to feed four cowhands in her kitchen all the time. Chad just laughed at her and went to change for the social. He had decided not to let Sam's prejudice against his father stand in the way of what could be a pleasant evening in the company of a beautiful woman. Not intending to treat Sam as the enemy, Chad felt that Sam was a fair man who would be willing to admit he was wrong when Chad explained his father's side of things.

After leaving his horse at the livery stable and renting a buggy, he arrived at the Farris house shortly before seven. He had rented the buggy because he wanted to sit beside Miss Melody Grant as he escorted her to the schoolhouse, even though it was only a short ride. Of course, if it hadn't been for that fire, he would have had a much nicer buggy to take her in, but surely Sam had told her about the fire.

Twelve

While Chad was renting a buggy, Melody was pacing back and forth in her room at the Farris house. The past week had been the longest in her life. She had come riding into town after dawn on Monday, telling the hostler a lie about taking Fortune out for a little ride before sunrise. Although she knew he could see that the horse had been ridden farther than just a short way, she was too shaken to care what he thought. She had also had to lie to Sam and Lenore, who were already in the kitchen having breakfast, when she came in the back door. She did care what they thought, but she couldn't think of any other explanation for what she was doing out so early except to say that she had been riding. All through breakfast, she had felt as though they could see right through her and knew what she had done.

All the times she had thought about burning down some of Winslow's ranch, she had never expected to feel like this about it. One thing for sure, she would be a lot more careful before she did anything else to hurt him—if she did do anything else. The thought of helplessly watching those beautiful horses burn to death or being responsible for injuring Winslow's sweet housekeeper was enough to take the taste of revenge out of her mouth for a long time. Then, when she had seen Chad with his hand all bandaged, she had actually felt sick to her stomach. Standing so close to him, she was sure he could tell that she was the one responsible for his burn.

Why in the world, she thought, did I let Lenore talk me into going to this social with Chad? She did have a vague notion that she could make up some for what she had done by being nice to him. Feeling as though she were doing penance, she hadn't allowed herself to look forward to the evening ahead. Still, she had taken a great deal of care to look her best.

She looked out the window in time to see Chad pull up in front. Momentarily confused to see him with a buggy, she quickly realized that he could have rented it at the livery stable. Darn, she said to herself, why does he have to be so good-looking?

Lenore's knock interrupted her thoughts. "Melody, Mr. Winslow is here," she said, sticking her head in the door.

"Come on in," Melody replied, looking at herself in the looking glass in the corner. "I'm about ready. How do I look?"

"You look beautiful enough to pop his eyes out."

"Tell me, Lenore, why are you so set on pairing me off with a Winslow? I thought you didn't care for that bunch."

"Well, I don't like his father much, but Sam says Chad is different. Besides, he is going to be a very rich rancher and a lawyer, too. A girl could do worse."

Melody didn't bother to answer, busying herself with her hair. Since she had chosen not to tell Lenore about her fiancé in St. Louis, she really didn't have a good reason not to see Chad Winslow. Anyway, it was just for one night.

When she came down the stairs and into the parlor, Sam and Chad were deep in conversation. When Chad saw her, he rose and came toward her, forgetting all about his talk with Sam. Taking her hand, he stared into her eyes making her heart flutter. Suddenly it was as if there were no other people in the room—in the world— except the two of them. They stood as though rooted to the spot until Sam broke the spell by saying, "We had best be going if we plan on being there in time for the first dance."

Lenore again checked all the children to see that they looked respectable, which gave Chad and Melody time to get out the door before the others. Soon, they were riding along in the buggy side by side. Melody liked riding next to him behind the high-stepping horse, with the evening breeze playing with her hair which hung long and lustrous in curls down her back. It seemed as if they arrived much too soon at the schoolhouse.

They created quite a stir when they arrived. There was no doubt that the tall, dark young man and the comely flaxen-haired schoolteacher made a very striking couple. Melody had kept herself aloof from most of the social doings since she had been in Marysville, and people were surprised to see her escorted by Chad Winslow. There had been a great deal of curiosity about the young Mr. Winslow since his arrival back in town. At first, some people were uncomfortable with him around, but his easy manner soon put most of them at ease. Then, too, Sam and Lenore were very popular with everyone, and it was plain that they liked this young man.

The remainder of the evening was almost like a dream

to Melody. Chad was everything she had ever wanted in a companion; witty, intelligent, charming, attentive. The fact that he didn't know many people made it possible for him to spend most of his time with her, but it was obvious, even to her, that he wasn't interested in anyone else. They danced and laughed and ate and talked as if the evening had been planned just for them. Afterwards, Chad took her home by a rather long route, which she didn't mind at all, not wanting the evening to end. Back at the Farris house, they sat on the back porch talking about his college days, while he held her hand gently in his. For a moment, as they said goodnight, she wondered if it would be proper to let him kiss her, but he simply ran the back of his hand slowly down her cheek—then was gone. The almost reverent gesture left her more shaken than a kiss would have.

Melody was glad to see that everyone was in bed when she went up the stairs to her room; she didn't want to break the spell by talking to anyone.

As Chad rode whistling toward home, Melody sat in her room wondering when she would see him again. She had mentioned that her children would be having a program next Friday night to mark the end of school. Hoping that he would attend, she also hoped that she wouldn't have to wait a whole week before she saw him again.

While Melody was wondering how long it would be before she saw Chad, he was trying to think of a good excuse to ride into town during the coming week. Anyway, he intended to escort her to the program on Friday. For one thing, unlike his father, he intended to become an active member of the local community. In fact, when he had built up a proper law practice, he wanted to build a large house in town. After the railroad came through Marysville, it was bound to grow, and he wanted to be there to help see that it became a first-rate town with more class than Silver City, for example. For now, he just wanted to get to know the local people and be known by them.

Of course, his main reason for going to the program at the school was the chance to see Melody again. He had never enjoyed an evening in a young lady's company as much as he had enjoyed this evening. Every time he saw her, he found out something different about her. The cultured, mannerly young woman who had floated around the floor in his arms tonight bore little resemblance to the free-spirited girl that had accepted Marty's challenge to jump the fence. Her speech and manner revealed a high-class bringing-up. In fact, she reminded him in many ways of his southern relatives. There was little doubt that his mother would have approved of the Melody he had been with this evening, but she would have been horrified to see a women dressed in pants and riding like Melody did. Yet he had to admit he was as fascinated with that side of Melody as with the more ladylike side.

His mind full of thoughts of Melody, he rode along hardly aware of the miles he had covered. Suddenly, a shot rang out. Chad slipped quickly to the ground, drawing his gun; in the dark, he didn't have a target to shoot at. A slurred voice called out, "Who ar' ya an' what ar' ya doin' here?"

Chad moved around, putting Beau between him and the grove of trees where the disembodied voice came from. Then he answered, "I'm Chad Winslow, and this is my land. That's what I'm doing here. Who the hell are you?" The agitation was clear in his voice and in the unaccustomed use of profanity. He was too angry at being challenged on his own land to be really frightened.

A strange sound almost like a giggle came from the man who weaved into view. It was an ugly sound coming from a man, but then it came from an ugly man. Chad hadn't noticed the first time he saw Frank just how ugly he was. Now, his insipid grin showed but a few teeth, all of them a putrid yellow; his grey beard showed that he hadn't shaved in days. As he came closer, the odor mixed with the smell of whiskey bore mute testimony of the length of time since he had bathed. He said, "Whatta ya know 'bout that? Almost shot th' big-shot lawyer."

"You stupid fool, what are you doing out here taking potshots at people?" Chad slid his gun into its holster.

Frank's grin turned to a look of bewilderment. "Jest doin' what th' ol' man said. Shootin' first—askin' questions later."

As Chad moved around Beau toward Frank, he said, "I'm sure my father didn't mean for you to be drunk when you were guarding the place. Without that whiskey, even you should be able to tell the difference between an intruder and someone who belongs around here. I think you had better go back to the bunkhouse and sleep off the whiskey before you do something else stupid." He reached his hand out and said, "I'll take that rifle."

"Seein' as how it's yore ol' man's, I guess I ain't got no choice." He lightly tossed the rifle to Chad, who caught it and held it by the barrel.

"I think you better give me your gun, too, until you're sober enough to be trusted with it."

Even watery with whiskey, Frank's eyes flashed a danger signal. As his shaky hand fumbled for his gun, he growled, "Reckon you'll jest have t' take it, if you want it so damn bad."

"Right!" Chad swung the rifle butt against Frank's temple, knocking him to the ground in a limp pile. Then, he casually removed Frank's gun from where it had dropped.

"What's goin' on here?" Ed said as he and Bob rode up. "We heard th' shot an' figured Frank had spotted someone snoopin' 'round. Sure didn't expect it t' be you."

"He's so drunk, he doesn't even know what he's doing. The rest of you haven't been drinking, have you?"

"Nah, Chad. We've been 'round here long enough t' know that you don't drink on Winslow property. Frank has been nothin' but trouble since th' boss sent him back here. He's got th' idea that th' boss thinks he's somethin' special."

After Bob got Frank's horse from the trees, the three men draped Frank over the saddle. Chad gave Frank's gun to Ed with instructions to give it back when Frank was cold sober and not before. "If he has anything to drink around the bunkhouse, get rid of it. If he gives you any trouble when he comes to, let me know."

"Usually, he's easy enough t' handle when he sobers up. He ain't got no guts at all 'less he's 'most blind drunk," Bob said, and Ed agreed.

The men mounted and rode in silence to the bunkhouse. Chad wondered what his father would have to say about Frank's behavior. When Mary Winslow was alive, no one was allowed to drink at the ranch. That was one of the reasons H. J. had invested in Sally's place, figuring it would give the men somewhere to drink that was far enough away from the ranch to suit his wife. As Chad got older, he had wondered if his dad's relationship with Sally had been purely a business one; now that his mother was gone, he didn't think it mattered much. If she had lived with it all those years, it sure wouldn't hurt him to.

Anyway, that had nothing to do with the problem at hand. He didn't much like the idea of having Frank around after tonight's scene, but he could send Frank back out to work with Marty until H. J. got back. Then he hoped he could convince H. J. to fire Frank like he should have in the first place.

As the men deposited Frank on a bunk, Chad said, "On second thought, I'll just keep his gun. When he comes around, tell him I want to see him."

Chad wiped Beau down himself, then turned him into the pasture. He went into the house and straight up to bed, not looking forward to his confrontation with Frank. He had the uneasy feeling that Frank would spell big trouble before it was over. One thing for sure, Frank had created a sour end to a lovely evening.

Thirteen

"*They said* ya wanted t' see me, Mr. Winslow," Frank said with sarcasm. The men had thrown him in a tub of cold water partly to sober him up and partly to clean him up, but Chad noticed that it didn't improve matters much. Still a stinky, grimy man, Frank didn't even have sense enough to feel out of place, standing in the spotless entryway to the elegant house.

"Yes, Frank, I did want to see you. Since you appear to be more in command of your senses, I will give this back to you." Chad handed Frank his gun. "However, I expect you to be more careful whom you shoot at from now on."

"I was jest doin' what th' ol' man said."

"My father didn't tell you to get drunk. I'll tell you right out that if it was up to me, I would fire you. I don't think we need your kind around here."

Frank started to protest, but Chad ignored him. "Now, I don't want you around the house anymore. If you still want to work for the Winslows you go back out to Marty and tell him I sent you to work for him. I can help the other men keep an eye on things around here."

Chad opened the door, and as Frank brushed past

him, Chad said, "I guess you know enough not to draw on Marty. He can drop you before you even have your gun free."

Frank muttered, "He don't scare me."

"I didn't think he did. A man has to have some sense before he can be afraid of anything." Chad closed the door firmly before Frank could reply. He was aware that he had made himself a dangerous enemy, but Frank was such a fool that Chad didn't figure he would be much trouble to deal with when the showdown came. Frank needed the money he could make working around here for a while; so, he would probably go back to Marty, who would keep him busy for some time. Now that Frank was taken care of, Chad could go back to figuring a reason to see Melody before Friday.

This week had been a trying one for Melody; the children were jittery about the program for Friday, and excited about the last week of school. The weather was so beautiful that everyone, including Melody, wanted to be outdoors, and she was having a great deal of trouble keeping her mind on school. Every time she heard a horse or a footstep, she looked expectantly at the door, but it was never Chad.

On Wednesday, she was walking home after school when she saw H. J. riding around town. The sight of him sent a shiver down her back. With him rode a man who would never be mistaken for a cowhand. Not one to make snap judgements, she had to admit that this man was, without any doubt, a hired gun. She had heard stories about men whose very look could make your blood run cold, but she had never believed them until now. Beside H. J. rode one—the ugliest man she had ever seen.

He was huge, dwarfing one of Winslow's largest

horses. His hair was long and black, hanging below his shoulders; his nose was large and hawk-shaped. As they rode past her, he looked at her with the coldest eyes in the whole country. They were grey-white, with no expression of any kind—almost as if there was no life behind them. As the two men rode through town, people instinctively moved closer to the buildings as if afraid to let even his shadow touch them. H. J. was obviously making sure that everyone saw the two of them, because they rode down the main street a couple of times before heading north out of town. Melody thought of H. J.'s ad about shooting anyone who trespassed on his property, and she knew that this was a man capable of carrying out that threat.

Shaken by the sight of the strange man, she decided to stop and visit with Sam for a minute before going home. She didn't like to alarm Lenore, who took everything as a personal threat to Sam, worrying about him the way she did. As Melody opened the door of the newspaper office, she caught sight of a very agitated Chad, who was practically shouting at Sam. At first she thought that Chad was angry with Sam, but as she listened, she realized, to her relief, that he was raving about his father.

"If I had known why he wanted me to meet the stage, I never would have come!" He had his back to Melody and hadn't heard the door open. "Some guy shows up at the house, says my ol' man paid him to ride out and tell me to meet the afternoon stage with a couple of horses, so I did. I had no idea he had done something so stupid. Matt Slade—he went and hired Matt Slade."

"Who's Matt Slade?" Melody asked quietly.

Chad turned around with a startled look which quickly melted into one of delight as he took in her radiant smile.

His tone of voice changed abruptly as he said, "I doubt if a lady like you would have heard of him, but most folks, even in the East, know that he is the meanest killer around. He doesn't bother much with talk or the law. Anyone who gets in his way is dead—period."

Melody went a little white at the thought that H. J. had hired this man because of her. Chad, thinking he had frightened her, quickly changed the subject. "Well, one good thing has come out of this. Since I am in town, would you care to take a ride with me? You do have your horse at the stable, don't you, Melody?"

Pleased to hear him use her first name, she smiled and said, "Yes, I keep Fortune at the stable, and I would love to go for a ride."

"I have to discuss something with Sam. That'll give you time to change, and I'll meet you at the stable in about a half hour."

After she had changed into a divided skirt, shirt and riding boots, she went to the stable, and had Fortune saddled and ready by the time Chad joined her.

He seemed pleased that she was ready. "I don't know how proper it is to meet a lady at a stable, but I thought you might like to ride your horse."

"Don't apologize. I love to ride Fortune. I always hated to ride in St. Louis because my uncle insisted I ride side-saddle. Once in a while I would sneak off and go riding in the country. That is one thing I definitely prefer about the West; women are freer out here to be themselves without so many airs."

"I hadn't thought about it much, but it does seem like it, doesn't it? I suppose in a way everyone is. Which is the reason a lot of men come out here in the first place, but too much freedom sometimes leads to trouble."

They were soon out in the open country, and they both enjoyed the afternoon. Chad was pleased that she rode well enough to keep up with him. In fact, she seemed to enjoy showing off Fortune, occasionally jumping something just to prove that she could. The horse was impressive, but the rider was what kept Chad's attention.

When they arrived back in town, there was a message at the stable for Chad to come to the Farrises' for supper. To their great happiness, they got to spend another couple of hours in each others' company. Even though Sam and Lenore were a few years older, Chad and Melody both liked them a great deal, and the two couples had a lot to talk about.

Friday evening, just as he had promised, Chad arrived early in order to get Melody to the school before anyone else arrived. This was to be the first school program that they had ever had in Marysville, and everyone with children in the school was looking forward to it. Since the night was a bit chilly, Chad started the fire in the little pot-bellied stove. Then, he and Sam set some extra chairs and benches around the room. As the students arrived, Melody seated them on two rows of benches across the front of the room, facing their parents and friends. At first, the children were nervous, and Melody, acutely aware of Chad watching her, was even more nervous. However, as the evening went on, everyone relaxed. Melody had given each student something to memorize or a part of a lesson to recite, and she was well pleased at how well they all did.

After the program, the women served refreshments. Chad and Melody, being the only single couple there, received a great deal of good-natured kidding, and finally, they were escorted to their buggy while the other adults put everything back in order. They rode even farther than before, and this time when he said good night, Chad kissed her gently.

Her head in a whirl, she hoped that Sam and Lenore would be asleep as they had been the last time. Her cheeks were burning, and she was sure they would guess why. However, they were both waiting for her in the parlor.

Lenore said, "Would you sit down a minute, dear? Sam has some news for you."

Melody reluctantly sat down as Sam said, "Everyone was very impressed with what you've taught the children in such a short time. The school board had a brief meeting after you left, and we voted unanimously to offer you another term as our teacher."

Melody hadn't planned to be around that long, but who could tell what was going to happen now? She said, "Thank you. I'm very happy that you were all pleased with my work. I'll have to think about it some."

"Tell her the rest, Sam," said Lenore.

"Lenore and I have been talking about what you will do during the recess, and we wonder if you would like to stay with us. You are so much help and company for Lenore, it won't put us out any. Also, we know how hard it must be to move around from family to family while school is in; so we told the board that we wanted you to stay right here with us the whole time."

Lenore interrupted, "During the time you have been with us, we have come to think of you as family. We would be so happy to have you stay here."

Melody was very touched by their kindness, especially since it meant she would be able to stay in town for a while. Right now, she was very happy being right here.

For the next few weeks, Chad and Melody spent more and more time together. They took long rides on Beau and Fortune, ate picnic lunches by singing streams, walked in the moonlight, and kissed on the Farris back porch. It was a happy time for Melody. For the first time since she could remember, she felt free of the driving desire for revenge. Somehow, when she was with Chad, it didn't matter who his father was or what he had done. Everything seemed quiet in the valley. Once in awhile, Slade and Winslow would show up at Sally's, but other than that no one ever saw them. Chad never spoke about Slade to Melody.

Mostly they talked about pleasant things. She told him about growing up in St. Louis. Carefully avoiding any mention of her early years, she said simply that her father had died when she was eleven—never saying how. He told her about his mother, and despite the image she had carried of a haughty woman, she found that she liked the woman Chad painted. He shared his plans for the future: his part in the growth of Marysville, the way he would run the ranch, and his dream of seeing a valley and a state where men took care of their differences through the courts instead of with violence. She especially loved to hear him talk about his plans. His valley would be a good place to live.

Many nights as she lay awake thinking about him, she wondered how things would have been had her family stayed here; would she have met Chad and fallen in love and been married? The cattle baron's son and the nester's daughter—what a match that would have been. When Chad spoke of his mother, Melody wondered if she hadn't had the schooling and advantages she had in St. Louis, would he have found her attractive? Strange how she had hated so much of her life in St. Louis, and yet, it was that life that helped make herself the young lady who had attracted him. For that she would always be thankful.

One afternoon, as Chad and Melody were out riding in Chad's new buggy, they saw two riders approaching in the distance. Melody got a sick taste in her mouth at the sight of H. J. and Slade. She had refused to think about H. J. at all. Since Chad was aware of her aversion to his father, he had never taken her to the main house when H. J. was around. It was hard for her to sit still as the two men pulled up. The combination of a man she hated and a man she feared was overpowering, and she had a strong urge to flee.

Chad stopped the horse and spoke quietly to his father, ignoring Slade as he had done ever since Slade had arrived. "Dad, have you met Melody Grant? She is the schoolteacher in town, and a very good friend of mine," he said, smiling at Melody with pride.

Highly impressed with the beautiful young lady sitting beside his son, H. J. tipped his hat and said, "Well, I'm very glad to finally meet you. We've heard a great deal about you around our place." The last wasn't exactly true since Chad hadn't been talking to his father much about anything—especially not Melody. To Chad, H. J. said, "Why don't you bring the young lady around for supper sometime?"

"Maybe, someday. Right now I don't think I want her around the company you're keeping these days."

H. J. followed Chad's gaze toward Slade, who was a little way behind him, and his eyes flashed anger for just a moment before he decided not to make a scene in front of the lady. From what little he had heard from Rosie and some of the hands, this Miss Grant just might be the kind of woman who would make a suitable mother for his hoped-for grandsons. Composing himself, he said, "Well, son, maybe things will be different soon. Everything has been quiet since I hired Slade. You have to admit that."

"Yes, well, we are planning on riding quite a ways today, so we had better be going."

"How 'bout doin' somethin' for me while yore out? If you stay on this road and bear to the left at the fork, you can drive up to within a half mile or so of the dam. I need to know what kind of condition it's in, and how much water is still flowing through there. It looks like a dry summer." He tipped his hat again to Miss Grant and rode off before Chad had a chance to answer.

Same ol' dad, Chad thought to himself. Never asks—just tells. He shrugged and smiled at Melody. "Oh, well, it will be a different ride anyway. Do you mind?"

Still a bit shaken, Melody just nodded. It was a strange turn of events. A few weeks ago, she had planned on asking Chad to show her this dam, and now, when it didn't matter to her, she was going to see it—by H. J.'s order, no less.

As they rode along, Chad talked about the atmosphere at the ranch since Slade had been hired. "Marty goes around with a frown most of the time. Most of the other hands know Slade by reputation and stay clear of him. Only one of them, Frank Smith, has had much to say about his presence. Did I tell you about Frank?"

"Isn't he the man who picked the fight with Sam?"

"He's the one. He's a stupid man who never seems to learn." He told her about his encounter with Frank which surprised her somewhat.

"Did you have to hit him like that?" she asked.

"It was either that or shoot him, and you can't shoot a

man just for being stupid."

Melody frowned at the idea of Chad shooting someone, but then another thought took its place. "What about now? Aren't you worried that he might try to get back at you?"

"He has been carefully avoiding me. Right now, he has something else on his mind. Apparently he thought that when my father got back, H. J. would give him back his job guarding the place. For some reason it had given him a sense of importance which Slade's presence took away from him. Even Frank isn't foolish enough to openly challenge Slade, but he has been doing a lot of bragging about how he could easily take Slade."

"I would think your father would fire him for shooting at you!"

Chad laughed a little self-consciously. "To tell the truth, I never told him about it. We haven't been talking much lately. Besides, I've had my mind on more pleasant matters."

Melody blushed as he leaned over and squeezed her hand. After that, the talk turned to more pleasant things. When they reached the end of the trail, Chad helped her down, and they walked to the dam site. They were both shocked to see how low the water was. They had been enjoying the clear days so much that they had forgotten that crops and animals need rain. It looked like there was a dry summer and fall ahead, and a warning bell went off in Melody's head as she realized what that meant to a dozen or so small landholders who depended on water from this channel.

Chad said, "It doesn't look like there will be much water coming through here this summer."

Melody felt the anger rise in her. "What about the people who need this water to survive? Your father can spare some of it. He can always move some of his stock up higher if he has to."

"This is his land and the water is rightfully his. Those other people shouldn't have set up their places in an area where the water is so unsure. After all, Winslow cattle need water, too."

"Winslows can also absorb a loss a lot better than anyone else in this valley. What's ten or twenty head to your outfit? To some of these men, it is the difference between making it or going broke. Don't you care?"

"Yes, but I care a lot more about my father and about Marty. Marty's a good man who wouldn't let innocent people pay the price of one man's greed as you seem to see my father's motives."

Melody was really angry now, and the anger that was plain on Chad's face only added to her ire. "So, you and your ol' man are just alike after all," she shouted.

Something in the fire in her eyes got to Chad and he reached to touch her, saying soothingly, as if to a small child, "Come on, Melody, don't worry your pretty head about it. Women shouldn't get upset about things they don't understand." Instantly, he could see that he had said the wrong thing, but he wasn't sure why. His mother had never questioned anything that his father did; he never thought women cared about ranch business.

Melody started down the hill, so angry that she wanted badly to hit Chad, but she knew that he could drop her with one blow. Her uncle had always told her never to strike a man unless she was prepared to be hit back. She stalked all the way back to the buggy with Chad vainly trying to make small talk. Refusing his hand, she climbed into the buggy. As he stepped in and took the reins, she said to him in a terse manner, "Because I am in the middle of nowhere and have no other way to get home, I will have to ride with you. However, I want no conversation with you."

They rode in silence the long distance back to the Farris house. It was a much longer ride than it had seemed before. At her door, she jumped out before he could even get out to help her. She went in slamming the door behind her, without saying a word.

The argument with Melody had shaken Chad, but he had the feeling that her mood would pass. Up until this time, they had gotten along so well that he found it hard to believe she would be mad for long. He should have realized that she wasn't like his mother. She was part of a new generation of women who felt they had a right to an opinion about everything. Actually, it had been one of the things that had made her so attractive to him.

As he rode into his yard, he caught sight of Frank helping stack the lumber for the new carriage house. They had rebuilt the barn first, figuring it was the more important of the two burned-out structures. It was easy to see that Frank didn't like his task much, and the griping he was doing was wearing down the other men. Swinging down off Beau, Chad decided that as soon as his father got back from town, he was going to have to tell him about Frank. He led his horse into the new barn and into his stall. Rubbing the horse down gave him something to do to keep his mind off his fight with Melody, and even more, from wondering what his father would say about the water situation and about Frank.

Fourteen

"*Why* in tarnation didn't you tell me this before?" H. J. said. He and Chad were relaxing with their coffee after supper, and Chad had just finished telling him about Frank's shooting at him.

"I haven't seen a whole lot of you lately—at least not alone, and I don't like discussing ranch business with Slade around."

"All you have to do is tell me you want to talk to me, and I can send him out—just like I did tonight," H. J. said as he refilled his cup from the pot Rosie had left them. "So what did Frank say when he saw who it was?"

Chad told him the rest of the story, and when he got to the part where he hit Frank with the rifle, H. J. started to laugh. "I'll be danged. I didn't know you had it in you, son. Really flattened him, huh? He seems to have recovered all right."

Chad smiled at his father's laughter. It was good to be with him when he wasn't angry. "Being so drunk probably helped."

"Probably went down limp as a rag."

"Yeah, anyway, the reason I told you this is because I

feel that Frank spells trouble and should be fired. Now. Today when I came home, he was doing very little except griping. You can ask Marty about him. Frank isn't much of a hand—and he is a first class troublemaker. He's still fighting with the other men over that incident with Sam Farris."

H. J. frowned at the mention of his old enemy. He said, "Well, any man who hates Farris can't be all bad. Still, I don't like anyone taking potshots at my son. I'll see to him."

"I think everyone around here will be glad to see him go."

H. J. nodded, then abruptly changed the subject. "I was very impressed with your young lady, although she didn't say much. You know, I'm not getting any younger. It's about time I had some grandsons to carry on the family name."

"I haven't known Melody that long, Dad. Give me a little time." Chad was uneasy talking about Melody with his father. He changed the subject to the water situation. As he had hoped, his father got so involved in discussing the water that he forgot about Melody.

The next day, H. J. called Frank into his office. Frank swaggered in and dropped into the most comfortable chair, acting as though he had been there before. H. J. frowned at the way the man made himself at home, but decided to let it pass. "My son tells me that you took a shot at him."

Instantly, Frank's whole attitude changed; he sat up on the edge of his chair and said nervously, "I didn't shoot at him—jest int' th' air. I was jest lookin' out fer things. Like ya said."

"He seems t' think I should fire you—says you're trouble. Marty's been after me about it, too."

"Marty jest don't like no one 'round here what can draw as good as him," Frank shot back.

H. J. sneered at Frank as if realizing for the first time what a fool the man was. For a moment, he wondered if Frank could be trusted at all. "Don't be a fool! Marty can outdraw anyone on this ranch—except maybe Slade, and I wouldn't want to bet against him, even then." For a moment his eyes got a faraway look, as if he were thinking of something that happened long ago.

Frank nervously shuffled his feet, and the noise brought H. J. back to the present. "I was sorry t' hear that your little fight with Sam Farris turned out so bad. I figured you'd wipe the place up with him. Guess I underestimated him—or overestimated you."

Frank began to whine, "That weren't my fault. I told ya afore, jest give me another chance at 'im. I'll show ya. I'll show 'em all." A cruel animal anger glinted in his eyes.

H. J. smiled to himself. It was that cold hatred he had sensed in Frank that had caused him to single the man out in the first place. "Okay, Frank, I'm goin' t' give you a chance t' redeem yourself. Right now, I don't want you t' tangle with Farris. I'm goin' t' make Marty and Chad happy by firin' you."

Frank started to protest, "But, ya said. . ."

"Hold on a minute, man. I'm still payin' you, but from now on I want you t' hang around in town. I want t' know everythin' that is goin' on in that town. Especially what Sam Farris is up to. Slade or I will be in every few days t' check. If you need t' get hold of me in the meantime, you can send Sally's bartender out here with a message. You understand?"

"Not exactly. How am I goin' t' know what Farris is

doin'?"

"You can see, can't you? Sally knows everything that goes on in that town—everything she cares to, anyway. Tell her I want t' know. Also, I want you t' tell everyone that I fired you. I don't want anyone but Sally t' know that you still work for me. Got that?"

"Yeah. Gettin' paid fer hangin' 'round Sally's is my idea of a good job."

When Frank came out of H. J.'s office, he wouldn't say anything except that he had been fired. Chad and Marty were both relieved to see him ride out, but Chad still had the uneasy feeling that he hadn't seen the last of Frank Smith.

For Melody, the last two days had been endless. She hadn't fully realized how much Chad meant to her until she faced the possibility of not seeing him again. Feeling very sorry for herself, she went to answer the front door. Her heart gave a leap at the sight of Chad, hat in one hand, and a large bouquet of flowers in the other hand. Before she could say anything, Chad spoke. "Melody, I have something to say, and I hope you will let me say it before you shut the door on me."

Melody took the flowers Chad handed her, and led the way into the parlor. When they were both seated, Chad said, "I'm sorry we had that quarrel. You mean a great deal to me, and I don't want to lose you because of something my father does. We have carefully avoided any talk about his activities up to now. Can't we just keep it that way? Someday, we will have a chance to run things around here, and then we can make changes. For now, let's just worry about ourselves."

Melody was so happy to see him that it wouldn't have mattered much what he said. All she cared about right now was how miserable she had been without him. She didn't know how realistic it was to build a relationship with him while ignoring who his father was, but she sure meant to try.

Things went on as before: days in the country, nights at the Farrises', or some gathering in town. Once in awhile, she would wonder what her mother would say about her seeing Winslow's son, but when she was with him, her mind was too full of happiness for anything else. Everything looked rosy for her until late one hot, dry summer afternoon.

She had returned from the store to find Lenore and Sam talking about how serious the water situation was. Sam was saying that H. J. had shut up the floodgate, and one family had already had to sell out to him. Melody had had her head in the clouds so much, she hadn't even known. When Sam realized she was there, he held out a letter. "Melody, this came for you today."

Recognizing her aunt's handwriting, Melody decided to read the letter in her room. Her aunt kept her up to date on how her mother was doing, but she hadn't written for some time. Melody sat in the chair by the window and wept as she read:

Dear Melody,
   I am very sorry to have to tell you that your mother passed on yesterday evening. The last few weeks she had been totally unreachable. She seemed to be living in the past when you all lived in the West. It was a blessing that she was released from her suffering. God bless you, child.

Love,
Aunt Alice

Looking again at the date on the letter, she realized that her mother had been dead almost two weeks. Two weeks that I spent with the son of the man who caused all mother's suffering, Melody rebuked herself. As she thought of her mother, she remembered again what she had come out here to do: to show her mother that she could get some kind of revenge against Winslow. But, like a woman, she had let her heart get in the way of what she had to do. Maybe her mother had been right—women couldn't do anything about the things that were done to them.

Something in her snapped at that thought. "There is so something I can do," she shouted aloud. Quickly changing into the men's clothes she had worn the night of the fire, she ran down the stairs. Finding no one in the kitchen, she left her letter on the table with a note telling Lenore to read it, and that she would be gone the rest of the day. She needed some time alone, she explained.

She rode Fortune hard, because she had a long way to go. Never thinking about cowhands or hired guns, she headed across the Winslow land for the old Chaffin place. There, in a back corner of the rotting cabin, she carefully uncovered the package she had hidden there early in the spring. She rode more carefully with her precious load, until, finally well after dark, she found her way to the hated dam. Two things filled her mind: the people who needed this water as much or more than H. J. did, and the woman who cried from the grave for revenge. She hadn't hurt much more than H. J.'s pride before, but with water as scarce as it was, she knew that if she could destroy the dam so he couldn't fix it, the others would have a chance to survive. Their survival would probably hurt Winslow more in the long run than the few head he might have to sell cheap.

She didn't have much light to work by, and she was annoyed at herself for letting her anger at Chad keep her from paying more attention when she had been here with him. She carefully unwrapped the dynamite that she had sweet-talked out of a miner. Since he had explained how to use it, she felt fairly sure of herself. Fumbling a little in the dark, she placed the sticks down along the base of the dam on the dry side. She was just wondering if the fuses were long enough to give her plenty of time to get away, when she heard Fortune nicker. For the first time, she realized what could happen if she were found out. She crept over to where Fortune was prancing around, and looked through the trees at the two riders who were coming toward her. Although she couldn't tell who they were at that distance, an image of Slade's cold eyes made a shiver run down her spine. With no time to light the fuses or retrieve the dynamite, she swung into the saddle and slapped Fortune with the reins. As if sensing her urgency, the horse lunged forward, putting as much distance as possible between them and the now-alerted riders.

Fifteen

Although Chad usually enjoyed Marty's company, he wasn't very happy being with him tonight. He had expected to spend the evening in town with Melody, but his father had had other ideas. In a rage over something Sam had printed about the water situation, H. J. was convinced that some hothead would blame him for the weather and try to do something to his dam, especially since they had found the gate removed once already. Insisting that Matt Slade had to stay with him, he told Marty and Chad to check things out at the dam. They had tried to convince him to wait until the next day, but he was determined that it be done now.

At first, they did very little talking, since both men were unhappy about the assignment. Marty deeply resented H. J.'s hiring Matt Slade, feeling that he was a polished gun himself who could take care of any trouble they had. He knew that H. J. considered him too soft and it galled him. Chad, on the other hand, was thinking about his missed opportunity to see Melody.

Marty looked at the lost look on Chad's face, and smiled to himself. "Reckon you hadn't planned on spend-in' the evenin' with me."

Chad smiled at his friend and said, "Well, no, I didn't, but you know I always enjoy your company."

"I know you've spent a lot of time in town, lately, and I doubt if it's t' see Sam Farris."

"As a matter of fact, I have seen quite a bit of Sam. Not all of my time has been spent courting Melody Grant. I've been meeting a lot of the local people, and even doing a little work once in awhile. I want to build up a good law practice, and I'll need more clients than just my father. You would be surprised at how many really nice people there are in this valley."

Marty just grunted at the last statement, and then said, "I had always hoped you would run the ranch. I couldn't stand t' be in a town fer more than a hour or so myself."

"Well, I guess I've spent a lot more time in towns than you have. I do love the open country and the ranch, but the ranch is the ol' man's—and yours. I want something of my own. Someday, I'll probably come out here and take over, but not now."

"The schoolmarm wouldn't have anything t' do with yore thinkin' would she?" Marty asked.

"I made that decision long before I came back here to stay, but I will admit that she has figured a lot in my thinking lately. It would be nice to build her a big house in town. Now that the church is almost finished, I know she will want to be able to go all the time."

"Yeah, I figured as much. I'll admit I ain't seen a more beautiful woman in a long time, an' she can sure ride."

Chad smiled at Marty's praise of Melody. "She isn't the only person who has affected my thinking," he said as the smile faded. "I'm finding it harder and harder to be around my father. Tell me the truth, Marty, is it just me?"

It was obvious that Marty didn't like discussing H. J., but he did finally say, "No, Chad, it isn't you. The ol' man is changin'."

"Is he, Marty? Or are we just beginning to see him in a different light?" Chad asked, not really expecting an answer.

For a while they rode on in silence until Chad asked about the water, and their talk turned to how bad the year had been, and about the condition of the cattle. They talked some more about Melody, and they laughed together about some women that Marty had known. Neither of them really expected any trouble. Things had been so quiet since the fire, they felt that whoever was responsible had used up all his anger and had just given up.

It was Marty who first spotted the rider hightailing it away from the dam. He motioned to Chad, who understood and started after the fleeing horse, while Marty went toward the dam. Not being able to identify the rider because of the distance between them, Chad still felt that he had seen the horse before. He pushed Beau to his limits, but the other horse, with a head start, was just too fast. Knowing that there was a fence straight ahead, he figured that the rider would have to slow down to find a way around—but to his horror, the horse stretched out and jumped the fence without losing the rider. Chad pulled Beau up and sat there stunned. He had only seen one horse do that before: Fortune, and he only did it with Melody riding.

"Dear God," he said, "not Melody." Then he began to calm down somewhat and decided that he was jumping to conclusions. After all, she could have been just out riding when their appearance had frightened her. Having convinced himself that that was the situation, and knowing that he could always find her if he needed to, he went back to see what Marty was doing. Marty was down in the dry river bed, and when he looked up, he was holding some dynamite in his hand. He asked, "Did you see who it was?"

Chad felt as if someone had hit him hard in the stomach. Deciding that he wanted to take care of Melody himself, he said, "The horse had too much of a head start. It looks like we got here just in time."

"Yeah, I guess the ol' man was right, after all. Go tell him what we found. I'll hang 'round fer awhile jest in case the guy decides t' come back. Have H. J. send a man to relieve me toward morning. We ought t' have someone here all the time until the water situation improves."

"Right." Chad was hardly listening. He knew that he had to make a trip into town tonight, but that would still give him enough time to send a man out here before morning.

As he rode into town, Chad thought about the first time he had seen Melody at the Chaffin place. She never had said what she was doing there, carefully sidestepping the question when Marty asked her. Most of the cut fences had been around that property and the Matthews place. She had also been to the ranch the day before the fire. In fact, he had shown her around, and she had been especially curious about the carriage house. And those small boot prints he had found leading from the carriage house—they probably hadn't been a boy's at all. He hadn't thought about it before, but a woman's boots would fit those prints. Of course he didn't think of it. Who would expect a well-bred lady to do anything like that? Her obvious hatred of his father must have something to do with it.

Arriving in town, he went first to the livery stable, where he found the hostler rubbing down a hot, sweaty Fortune. He practically ran to the Farris house where he knocked once on the back door and then barged into the kitchen. He shouted at a startled Sam and Lenore, "Where's Melody?"

At that moment, Melody walked into the room. She had been crying, but she seemed calm. "So, it was you chasing me."

Chad grabbed her arm twisting it in his big hand, as he said through clenched teeth, "What were you doing out there? What the hell were you doing?"

Sam started to get up, as though to free Melody, but she shook her head at him. "Sit down, Sam. It's all right. He has a right to an explanation." To Chad, she said, "If you'll let go of me and sit down, I'll explain the whole thing."

Lenore said, "Come on, Sam. I think we should leave them alone."

"No, stay. It's time you knew about me, too," Melody said.

Chad calmed down enough to release her arm and half-sit on a chair. Melody stood with her back to them for a few minutes before she turned around with a blank, unreadable expression on her face. "First of all, I'm not Melody Grant. Grant was my mother's maiden name. I'm Melody Chaffin, and my family used to live in that cabin where you first saw me."

In a flat emotionless voice, as if reciting something she had reluctantly committed to memory, she told them all that had happened to her family, including her mother's long illness. She explained how she had hoped that getting revenge on H. J. would help her mother. When she started to tell about the fire at the Winslows, Chad stopped looking at her, staring instead at his hands throughout the rest of her story. Telling how her mother's death had made her ashamed for letting her feelings for Chad interfere with her mission, she started to cry. Lenore went to her, putting her arm around her, and the silent encouragement helped Melody compose herself enough to finish telling what she was doing at the dam.

Realizing she was through, Chad said, without looking up, "I can understand you being hurt, but why, if you hated my father and Marty so much, did you have to involve me? Or was that part of your scheme to get even with the Winslows?" He looked at her then with cold eyes. "If so, you might as well know that it worked beautifully. I had even planned on asking you to marry me tonight. That ought to give you a good laugh." He got up and burst out the door, slamming it so hard that the house reverberated with the sound.

"No," Melody said to the door, "I didn't plan on either of us falling in love—but I did, too."

However, Chad was already halfway down the street. He retrieved Beau from the surprised hostler and rode for home. At the moment he wasn't sure with whom he was the maddest: Melody, for using him in her scheme; his father, for the Chaffin mess and for sending him to the dam, tonight; or himself, because he had still wanted to take Melody in his arms and console her. He was only pleased about one thing: that he had asked Marty about the Chaffins. Having heard Marty's explanation of what happened, he was able to hear her story without getting silly over it. Of course, it had been hard on her mother and her. He could see that, but couldn't she see that her father had caused most of the trouble by his stubbornness? He knew how badly Marty felt about shooting her father. "It was your father or mine," he cried at the sky.

When Chad got home, H. J. was impatiently waiting for him. He had barely gotten in the door when he was struck with the force of H. J.'s anger. "Where the devil have you been, an' where is that stupid foreman of mine? I've been waitin' half the night for you two."

Chad was in no mood to care about calming his father. "When you stop cursing at me as if I were a servant I'll tell you what happened."

Something in Chad's tone and the set of his jaw made H. J. back off a little. "All right, son. I've been worried about you. That's all. Where's Marty?"

Despite the fact that he rarely drank, Chad poured himself a straight whiskey, drinking it half-down before he answered, "He's staying at the dam until someone comes to relieve him. He seems to feel that there should be someone there for a few days." He swallowed the rest of his drink and poured another one.

"What the hell for? You're not telling me everything." H. J.'s voice started to raise again.

"Marty found some dynamite at the base of the dam. It seems we arrived in time to prevent someone from blowing it up."

H. J. went into a genuine rage at that. "Didn't I tell you someone had it in for me? You both said I was crazy. Well, who the hell is crazy now? If I hadn't hired Slade, they would've tried t' kill me by now."

Chad choked on his drink as a laugh started to work its way up his throat. What would his father say if H. J. knew that he had hired a killer to protect himself against a tiny woman. The unaccustomed drinks were making him sick; he decided to go to bed. As he started for the stairs, he said, "Don't forget to send a man out to relieve Marty. He doesn't want to leave the place unguarded. Personally, I don't think it's necessary."

H. J. was so wrapped up in his own thoughts that he didn't even notice the last remark.

Chad flopped on his bed, closing his eyes against the nausea. He wasn't sure whether it was caused by the whiskey or by Melody. Marty would probably tell H. J. about the rider leaving the dam, and he would want to know why Chad hadn't told him about it. Chad didn't know what he was going to tell his father, but he knew that he wasn't going to tell him about Melody. Any other time, it would have been Marty he would have gone to with his hurt. In fact, he had almost gone back there tonight. But how could he tell Marty that a man he had killed so long ago had come back to destroy them all? At least to destroy Chad—poor, foolish, lovesick Chad.

When Marty got back the next morning, he didn't even see H. J., figuring Chad had filled him in. When they did talk, they had other ranch business to discuss. It wasn't until the next afternoon that H. J. had reason to get all steamed up again.

Sixteen

H. J. had never been so angry. As soon as the cook had returned from town with the paper, H. J. had closed himself in his office with it. After awhile, he had shouted for Chad and Marty. Now, the two men were standing together trying to read the article H. J. had pointed out. It was difficult for them to concentrate because of H. J.'s cursing, but they finally got through it.

It has come to your editor's attention that a person, who will remain unnamed because of possible retribution, tried unsuccessfully to blow up a dam belonging to H. J. Winslow. The dam has been used in the past to divert water away from many of the spreads in our valley. With the loss of the much needed water, several landowners have been forced to sell out to Mr. Winslow. While this editor can not condone the destruction of another man's property, the incident does point out again the need for some decisive action on the part of all the people in this valley before there is a real tragedy.

There was a lot more; mention of some of the people who had been bought out by H. J., interviews with some of the people who were being hurt by the shutting-off of their water, an editorial about the use of violence, and more comments about the need for a full-time law officer in Marysville.

As soon as Chad put the paper down, H. J. asked, "You mister bright lawyer, what can I do about this outrage? Can I make him print a retraction?"

Chad sat down in a big leather chair across from H. J.'s desk. "First of all, a retraction wouldn't help, because everyone has already seen it. A retraction would only draw more attention to it. Besides, it looks like everything he said is the truth. You can't sue a man for printing the truth—no matter how much you dislike it."

"A fat lot of good it did me t' spend all that money gettin' you educated. All you ever do is tell me I can't do something. First Shorty; now this. I don't need no lawyer t' tell me what I can't do. I want t' know what I can do."

Chad shrugged and said, "I just told you what the law can do. I don't write the laws. What's so bad, anyway? Hasn't he written things like this before?"

H. J. pounded on the desk. "Can't you see that every time he gets closer to home? It was probably his stories that caused this person to attack my dam. I told you somethin' like this would happen when he started writin' about me keepin' the water to myself. An' what about that unnamed business? He is protectin' a criminal! That is, if there really is someone else. I wouldn't put it past Farris t' do this stuff just so he has somethin' t' write about."

Chad was beginning to get annoyed at his father's line of reasoning. "Don't be ridiculous. . ."

"Ridiculous, am I?" H. J. tore at the paper until he found what he wanted and shoved it at Chad. "In this editorial he goes back over the Chaffin people. That was so long ago that I didn't remember who he was talkin' about at first." He turned to Marty for the first time. "Remember that nut that tried t' kill me, Marty? Of course Farris didn't print anythin' about that. Jest claims I was responsible for two deaths. Blasted fool."

Chad himself wasn't very happy about the articles in the paper. His and Sam's relationship had been built on an unspoken agreement to stay away from discussing H. J. or his affairs. Chad felt as if Sam had turned against him, too, and it added to his sense of loss over Melody. Jerked back into the present conversation, he realized that his father was now venting his rage on Marty. "If you were the man you were back then, I sure as hell wouldn't have t' be worryin' about some jerk like Sam Farris! You always said you would risk yore life for me, anytime."

A hint of anger flared in Marty's eyes, but he spoke calmly as he said, "H. J., I don't think you need protection from Sam Farris. He doesn't even wear a gun."

"The hell I don't! He just wants t' take everythin' I own away from me. I tell you if it wasn't for Slade, some hot-head would've tried t' kill me by now." His face lit up as if he had found the answer to his problem. "I'll bet Slade wouldn't sit there an' tell me I can't do anythin'. He would find a way t' stop Farris."

"Dad, use your brains. Everyone in the valley knows that Slade works for you. If he tries anything, they will just have more reason to come down on you."

For the first time since he had called them in there, H. J. smiled, but it wasn't a pleasant smile. He looked pleased with himself as he said, "Well, then I guess I'll just have t' find someway t' get rid of that man without involvin' me. Maybe, I can find someone who has his own reasons t' hate Farris."

Before either of the other two men could question him, H. J. dismissed them as if they were children. Chad looked at Marty's calm face as they walked outside together. Again he was struck with the difference in the two men. "How do you keep yourself under control when he rails at you like that?"

Marty shrugged and said, "I once had a temper like his, but I learned—the hard way—that the combination of a quick temper an' a fast gun hand always leads t' trouble. If it hadn't been for H. J., I would've probably hanged by now—or died in the dirt somewhere. I've never forgot his help or the lesson. I can't afford a temper."

Deciding to leave the conversation there, Chad asked, "Do you think he would really try to do something to Sam?"

"Hard tellin'. Used t' think I knowed him. 'pears I was wrong." Marty started to walk away, but Chad put out his arm and stopped him.

"Wait a minute, Marty. You have to tell me what you mean by that. I've always thought you knew him better than anyone—even my mother. What makes you think you don't?"

"I didn't intend t' tell you this, but maybe I should jest in case somethin' happens." Marty stood with his thumbs in his belt, looking uncomfortable. "When you asked 'bout the Chaffins, it started me thinkin' about what happened. So I asked Kirk, who was with us then, what he remembered about them. He told me H. J. had given the orders t' stampede the cattle through the Chaffin place. They figured I knew. It seems there was at least two other times that H. J. gave orders t' run somebody off. Maybe yore friend Sam Farris knows the ol' man better 'n we do."

Chad felt his faith in his father slipping away from him. He studied Marty as if his face would tell him what he wanted to know. Finally, he said, "Blast it, Marty, if you know that, why are you still here?"

There was an air of resignation to Marty's voice as he

answered, "I told you. Yore ol' man gave me a chance t' lead a decent life. I owe him. The only thing I wouldn't do fer him is kill. I'll never kill again, except to save someone I care about. Like I've always told you, killin' a man does somethin' t' you. It either makes you so sick you never want t' do it again, or you like the feelin' of power it gives you—then you become a Matt Slade."

As Marty spoke his name, Slade appeared in the doorway of the house and called out, "Hey, Simpson, saddle th' boss's horse. He's goin' t' town."

Chad could feel the tension radiating from Marty, but his face wore no trace of anger as he calmly said, "I don't take orders from no hired gun."

Slade's gun hand moved as if jerked by an unseen string. He moved closer to Marty and stood with his legs apart as if about to draw. He snarled, "Yore talkin' like a man what plans on backin' up his words."

Marty stood poised and ready, but he answered quietly. "If I ever draw on you, Slade, it'll be the last thing you ever see."

H. J.'s irritated voice shattered the tension. "Where the hell is my horse? Marty, get Ed t' saddle my horse. I have t' go t' town on business."

Chad asked, "Is Slade going with you?"

"No, I've given him somethin' t' do."

Marty went into the barn and gave Ed the orders, then he saddled up and rode out. Slade went back into the house, and H. J. soon rode off toward town. Since it was the first time H. J. had gone into town without Slade since he had hired the gun, Chad was uneasy about it. H. J. was definitely up to something and it didn't look good. Chad decided that he would just take a little trip into town himself. Figuring his father wouldn't want him along, he waited long enough to give him a good head start before he followed, slowly. He figured whatever his father was up to would take him a little time to accomplish. H. J. couldn't get into much trouble before Chad caught up to him.

After Chad had left the Farris house, Melody had fallen apart. The grief of her mother's death, and the realization that she had lost Chad for good overwhelmed her, and she fell into a chair sobbing. Lenore brought her a wet cloth to wash her face and some hot tea to drink. After awhile she began to recover and looked closely at the two people she had grown to love like her own family. "You must think I'm an awful person, too," she said almost like a question.

Lenore started to reassure her, but Sam gave her a look which changed her mind. When she backed away, Sam pulled his chair over beside Melody and took her hands in his. Then he looked her in the eyes, and said, "Melody, we told you before that you are like family to us. I feel like your big brother; so, I'm going to talk to you like one. There is no doubt that the memories you have lived with all these years are terrible ones, and it is not hard to understand your desire to see H. J. pay for what he did. Especially since he seems to have gotten away with everything he did to your family—plus a lot more. Believe me, I've felt like taking vengeance on him myself before. Whenever I feel like that, there are two things that stop me. One is the realization that every story has two sides. Did you ever think, for instance, that maybe Marty was right when he said that they didn't know anyone had been hurt in the stampede? It could have been an accident."

"Even so, that wouldn't help my brother any."

"No, I'm not saying it would. Still, many people die because of another's carelessness. I don't think Marty Simpson would kill a man in cold blood. I've seen him walk away from a fight before—one he could have won."

"So Chad was always telling me." She winced a little as she said his name. "He really looked up to Marty. But still. . ."

"I know. Your father is still dead. That's where my second reason comes in; even if they are guilty, there is a right way and a wrong way to do things. Why do you think that I work so hard at the paper when it doesn't even make me a decent living? Because I believe the right way to seek justice is through the law and law-abiding people. This is a great place to live, and it will be better when we can show people like H. J. that violence is not the way to settle our problems. First, we have to be willing to live that way ourselves. We can't say 'no violence,' then go running around trying to solve our problems through violence."

Melody looked down at her hands for a minute, then said, "Everything you've said sounds really nice, but it doesn't help. All my family is dead—all in one way or another taken from me by Winslow." She began to cry softly.

Sam put his arms around her and just held her until the tears began to let up. Then he said, "If you can't accept anything else I've said to you, remember that in God's good time, H. J. will pay for what he's done. You can be sure of that."

"That's what my aunt used to tell my mother."

"She was right, Melody. Just think of what your need for revenge has gotten you," Sam said, standing up and stretching. "It's getting very late. I think we had better call it a night."

Later, in her room, Melody thought about what Sam had said. What had her desire for revenge gotten her? She was worse off than when she had started this whole thing. For the next two days she refused to come out of her room. She went over and over the whole mess in her mind, and all she could decide was that she hated H. J. more than ever. In one way or another, H. J. had cost her everyone she had ever loved. Now, he had cost her the one she loved the most. It was because of him that she would never see Chad again; she didn't know how she could live with that. She had to leave Marysville, but she couldn't go back to St. Louis. Even that was lost to her. She had written her fiancé and broken her engagement weeks ago, which was just as well, because she could never marry him after loving Chad. She hadn't known what it was like to really be in love before.

On Wednesday night, she was beginning to pack her things, planning on taking the stage out of town the next morning, when Lenore came to the door. "Melody, please let me in. I've brought you something to eat. You have to eat sometime."

Deciding it was time to let Lenore know her plans, Melody let her in. Lenore looked hurt when she saw that Melody was packing. Melody said, "I was going to come down and tell you in a little while. I'm leaving in the morning. I know it isn't a very nice thing to do to the school board, but I'm sure they can find someone else to teach."

"I wasn't worried about that. I was just thinking about you. Where will you go?"

"I can always find a job teaching somewhere. Anywhere but here. I'm going to miss you and the children, but I can't stay around here. There's nothing but bad memories for me here."

"Sam and I are going to miss you so much."

"Where is Sam? I want to talk to him before I go."

Lenore waved her hand toward Main Street. "He's at the paper, as usual."

As they talked, the sound of a fast-approaching horse caught their attention. Since the house was not on the main street, they usually heard a horse only if it was coming to their place. Melody involuntarily looked out the window. It was a Winslow, all right, but not the one she'd hoped to see. What was H. J. doing coming into town through this street? He rode on past going toward Main Street. Of course, he wouldn't be coming here, Melody thought. He probably doesn't even know who lives here. The sight of him stirred something in her: the realization of why all her schemes to get even with him had failed. She turned to Lenore and said, "Let me finish here, and I'll come down and eat with you."

After Lenore left, Melody stood at the window looking down the street. The reason she had failed was that she hadn't been thinking the way H. J. would have. She had been fooling around with petty things when she should have gone for the big prize. Only one thing would keep H. J. from ruining any more lives, she could see that now. He would have to be dead. Only then would she be free of him.

She didn't think about what would happen to her afterwards; she didn't care. If only he takes the same route leaving town, she thought. Quietly opening her door, she crept across the hall and into the Farrises' bedroom. She got down on her knees and felt around under the bed for the rifle that Lenore was always scolding Sam about. She wasn't as good a shot as Chad, but she could darn sure hit a target as big as Winslow.

Seventeen

H. J. had ridden into town down the side street so no one would be likely to see him. This way he could get in the back door at Sally's without going across Main Street. As he walked into the small room that served as an office for Sally and him, he was pleased to see her sitting behind the desk. He hadn't wanted to have to find her. She looked up and smiled at him. "How ya doin', boss? After readin' the paper, I kinda expected t' see ya showin' up here. Ya wanna drink?"

"No, I haven't got time. Frank still hangin' around?"

"Yeah, he's been here most of the time. Drinkin' too much an' makin' a nuisance of himself. If you hadn't said t' let him stay, I would have had him thrown out long ago."

"Get him in here. I don't want anyone else to know that I am here." H. J. sat down in the chair she vacated.

While she went after Frank, H. J. looked over the figures she had been working on. She was a pretty smart ole gal about some things. They were both making money off the place. Soon Frank's grimy face appeared in the doorway. At a nod from H. J., Sally closed the door behind him and went back into the main saloon. Frank looked even dirtier than usual, and he had had more to drink than H. J. would have liked. Staggering to the chair across from H. J., he grinned and just folded up into a sitting position.

H. J. said, "Do you think you're sober enough t' use yore gun?"

"I reckon I can still shoot better than most."

H. J. had seen Frank's draw, and although he was better than some, there were still a lot of men around who could outdraw and outshoot him. Of course, he had chosen Frank for his ability to bear a grudge—not his fast gun. He needed someone who wasn't a known gun but could hate enough to shoot a man in cold blood. Frank was his man—there was no doubt about that. "I'm goin' t' give you the opportunity t' make a lot of money, an' afterwards I want you t' leave these parts for good."

Frank was suddenly very alert. "What's a lot of money?"

"Five hundred dollars," H. J. answered, pulling the money out of his pocket and laying it on the desk.

Frank's eyes gleamed and he gave a low whistle. "Who do I gotta kill fer that much?"

H. J. smiled to himself. Maybe the man wasn't such a fool after all. "Of all the people in this valley, who would you get the most pleasure outa killing?"

That familiar animal light came into Frank's eyes, but he didn't say anything. Figuring that Frank was following him, H. J. went on, "I want it t' look like a grudge thing between the two of you. You go back int' the saloon an' give me plenty of time t' get out of town. Talk it up how much you hate him; how it's his fault that I fired you. Then go down t' the paper an' call him out. You don't have t' worry much about him, because he doesn't carry a gun."

He opened a drawer in the desk and took out a short barrel .32, and handed it to Frank. "After you shoot him, throw this beside him an' say he had it in his pocket, intendin' t' shoot you. You were just defendin' yoreself. Got it?"

"Yeah, 'cept what if someone else says he didn't have a gun?"

"First off, the only people around should be your fellow drunks. What do they know? Besides, there ain't no lawman around. By the time the U. S. Marshall gets here, you'll be long gone. You just make sure that plenty of people see you. I don't want there t' be any doubt that it was between the two of you. Understand?"

"Can I have the money now?"

H. J. nodded. "Just be sure that you don't flash it around out there. As soon as Farris is dead, I want you out of town. Slade and I will be back tomorrow to check."

Frank stuck the gun in his left hand coat pocket, stuffed the money inside his coat, and headed for the door. H. J. got up and moved toward the back door. Stepping outside, he mounted his horse and headed back out of town the way he came in.

When Chad rode into town, it was hard for him not to turn toward the Farrises' house. He felt like he might just owe Melody an apology considering his father's recent behavior, but for now, he had more important business. When he didn't see his father's horse tied in front of the newspaper office, Sally's or any other place on Main Street, he figured that it must be in back of Sally's. He had seen his father go in that way when he didn't want to be seen. Chad tied Beau down the street away from Sally's, and moved quietly along to the back of the saloon. Seeing light coming out of the window in the back office, he figured his father was in there. The window was too high for him to see in without being easily seen, and he had a feeling that he wasn't wanted in there. It was a strange thought to have about his father. Spying a flight of stairs running up the building next door, he decided that he could probably see in the window from there. Sitting on a stair about halfway up, he could see most of the room. He had expected to see his father; he was shocked to see Frank sitting across from him. Chad couldn't hear anything they were saying, but he saw his father take out a great deal of money and spread it on the desk. Frank sat up and leaned toward it. After a few mintues, H. J. handed Frank a gun. After Frank went back into the saloon, H. J. came out through the back door, walking quickly to his horse. He mounted and rode off in a great hurry. Chad hunched down, staying very still, but his father never even looked around.

Chad sat on the stairs a minute, trying to figure out what was going on. It wasn't like his father to give so much money to anyone. In fact, he rarely carried very much. Surely, his father had settled with Frank when he fired him. Anyway, they couldn't owe a cowhand that kind of money. Also, what was Frank doing with his father? Chad had seen Frank in town a couple of times after he had been fired, but he thought Frank was working for an outfit closer in. Tonight, he looked as if he hadn't been doing anything except drinking. His father had obviously come into town just to see Frank, but how did he know that Frank would be here?

Finally, he walked around to the front of Sally's and looked in the front window. Through the glare, he could see Frank at the bar doing a lot of gesturing with his hands. He was clearly upset about something and had a large audience for his complaints. Now Chad was sure he had to know what this man was up to, but he couldn't go into the saloon because he would be recognized. Walking around the corner of the building, he waited in the shadows where he could see anyone coming out the door. His father was surely on his way home; he didn't figure he needed to worry about him, for the time being anyway.

In her room, Melody checked the rifle to see that it was loaded and took up her vigil by the window. As she waited, a war was going on inside her. She remembered all the things Sam had said to her, but his words kept being interrupted by her mother's voice wailing for vengeance. Then she heard the faint clop of a horse's hoof. As it grew louder, she rested the rifle on the windowsill to steady it, and aimed the sights toward a spot in the middle of the street where she expected Winslow to pass. When he rode into view, she cocked the hammer back and felt her finger start to squeeze the trigger almost as if it was on its own. In a flash, the figure on the horse changed before her eyes, and she almost screamed as she thought she saw Chad riding toward her. The vision lasted only a second, but in that short time, H. J. had passed out of her sight. Trembling at what she had almost done, she knew that she loved Chad more than she hated his father. Even if she was capable of murder, she could never kill someone who belonged to Chad, no matter who he was.

She didn't know how long she sat there before she heard the shots. At first, she had the odd sensation that the gun in her hands had come to life and gone off on its own. Then she realized that the shots had come from Main Street and figured it was just some of the ruffians having themselves a little fun. It was strange that there were only three. Well, tomorrow she would be gone from here; maybe she could find a place where things were a bit quieter. She stirred herself from her thoughts and went back across the hall, carefully putting the rifle back in its usual place. She was walking back toward her room when she heard Lenore scream below.

Eighteen

Chad didn't have long to wait. Frank came swaggering out of the saloon, hollering at the men who were following him. "If ya don't think I can, jest follow me."

Chad was surprised to see Frank head back toward the main part of town, since he had guessed, with all that money, Frank would head for the brothels or the gambling house the other way. Instead, he seemed to be heading toward the newspaper office, with a trail of jeering drunks behind him.

Frank started shouting obscenities as soon as he got within shouting distance of the paper. Stopping in front, he called out, "I know you're in there, Sam Farris, you yellow-bellied snake. Come out here an' fight, if yore man enough."

Looking out and seeing Frank, Sam nonchalantly walked out, closing the door behind him. He smiled good-naturedly at Frank and said, "Go home, Frank. You're drunk," as if addressing a naughty child.

Frank posed himself with his feet apart, sweeping his dingy coat clear of his holster. "Ain't got no place t' go. Got fired 'cause of you. An' ya wanted my friend Shorty hanged. Well, ya got yore wish, but ya have t' answer t' me. Draw, if ya ain't afraid."

Finally realizing what was going on, Chad's last little bit of trust in his father broke inside him, leaving him empty of everything but anger. He quickly worked his way around the crowd where he could come up on Frank's right.

Sure that Frank was all talk, Sam just sneered at him and turned to lock his door. Chad didn't make the same mistake. As Frank's gun left his holster, Chad shouted "Watch it, Sam!"

Sam turned and felt Frank's bullet rip through his arm, knocking him against the building. At Chad's cry, Frank spun around to face him. Having anticipated his move, Chad drew and fired once. The bullet hit Frank square in the chest, twisting him around before he fell in the dirt— lifeless. Frank's gun went off by reflex, but the bullet just kicked up the dirt around him as he fell.

Chad went first to Sam who was leaning against his office, looking dazed. "I didn't think he hated me that much. I owe you, Chad!"

"You don't owe me anything. I was just paying a family debt." Chad walked over to Frank's still form. Kneeling beside it, he removed the blood-covered bills from Frank's coat, and carefully wrapped them in his handkerchief. Then he picked up the gun and said, "I'll just see that these get back to their owner."

Melody ran down the stairs and into the kitchen where Lenore's scream had come from. As she entered the room, Chad was easing Sam into a chair. Sam smiled at Lenore and said, "I'm all right. I was only hit in the arm."

Chad reassured her. "I looked at him before. Although I'm no doctor, I think the bullet just went through the muscle. Do you have something to clean it out with?"

Lenore started to tend to Sam's wound, but he said, "Chad can help me with that. You take the kids upstairs, and calm them down. Where's the baby?"

"She was asleep. I hope my scream didn't wake her." Gathering the other children around her, she headed for the stairs.

Melody silently brought Chad the things he asked for. With her help, Chad got Sam's shirt off and his wound cleaned and dressed. While they worked on him, Sam told Melody how Chad had saved his life, making Chad a real hero. Chad, looking at the bloodstains on his clothes, said quietly, "I'm no hero. Marty was right. Killing a person isn't something a man can take pride in. No matter what the reason."

Lenore came in, in time to hear some of the story. She handed Chad a wet rag to clean up with and said, "Maybe not, but I'm sure glad you were around tonight." She shuddered at how close her fears had come to being reality.

Melody watched Chad with troubled eyes. He gave up the hopeless job of getting any blood off his clothes, took his jacket off, laid it across a chair back and sat down beside Melody. He said, "I have to tell you that I was wrong about your folks, the dam, my father—everything. I haven't sorted it all out yet, but it looks like my father was responsible for a lot more than any of us realizes."

Melody put up her hand to stop him, saying, "No, Chad, I'm the one who was wrong. Hating your father has only brought me more grief and sorrow. I should never have tried to get my own revenge. I do want you to know that I didn't mean to use you. It just happened."

"Melody Grant—I mean, Melody Chaffin—I love you."

Melody touched the side of Chad's face and said, in that low voice that thrilled him, "I love you too, Chad Winslow."

"You know that is the first time I've ever heard you say my last name without a snarl," Chad said happily.

"Well, I learned tonight that love can be stronger than hate." She laughed at Chad's puzzled look, and said, "Someday I'll tell you about my evening."

Taking her hands in his, Chad said softly, "Tomorrow I'm going to Silver City. I should be back on Saturday. Do you think you could be ready to marry me on Sunday? Isn't this the Sunday the preacher has services?"

"Yes, this is his Sunday in Marysville."

"I know it is short notice, but I want to leave for the capital Sunday afternoon."

Melody smiled. "Oh, darling, it doesn't matter. The only people I care about are here. I would marry you tonight if you wanted."

"I have been rehearsing a proposal to you for quite a long time, and I didn't expect it to be like this. I know it wasn't very romantic, but I think you will all understand when I finish telling you what I've been planning all evening," he said, including the Farrises in the conversation.

Lenore got them all some stew and biscuits, and they ate as Chad filled them in on what he had learned since he had last seen them. It wasn't easy for him; eventually, he got it all out. "One thing, Melody, I want you to know. Marty really didn't know anything about the stampede that killed your brother. However, it wasn't an accident—H. J. planned it. I know that Marty killed your father, but he has a strong loyalty to H. J. Someday, maybe you can be able to forgive him."

"I'll try, since I know how much you care for him."

"The last thing you all need to know is about the business with Frank. I was there because I had been following him. You see, H. J. gave him that money to kill you, Sam."

Sam looked at Lenore. "I didn't realize H. J. hated me enough to kill me."

Lenore cried, "I told you he would do something awful if you didn't leave him alone. He'll just get someone else to do it for him now that Frank is dead."

Chad said, "Don't worry, Lenore. We're not going to let him hurt anyone else around here. I have some changes in store for him."

Turning to Sam, he said, "I'd like you to go to Silver City with me tomorrow. First, we could get a doctor to look at your arm, and I have to see Brady, who I understand is a friend of yours. He will probably better receive what I have to tell him with you along."

"I'll be glad to help as long as Lenore doesn't mind me leaving her alone."

Lenore was thinking that in Silver City he would be out of H. J.'s reach for a while, but she just said, "That's all right. Melody and I have a lot to do to get ready for the wedding. You men would just be in the way."

"I don't mean to push everyone, but I feel that the sooner we get this all done the better it will be for all of us. Sam, I want you to get every man in town and nearby to come to the schoolhouse tomorrow about eleven. There's not enough time to get the ones farther out, but we'll just have to get them later. That way we can make the afternoon stage easily."

Lenore and Melody started cleaning up the dishes while the two men talked about Chad's plans. Finally, Chad got up to go. "I have to see Sally about taking a message to H. J. for me, and then I'm going to get a room at the hotel for the night. I'll be here early in the morning to discuss the meeting."

He took Melody by the hand and led her out on the back porch. Taking her small face in his large hands, he said, "You remember the first time I kissed you was on this porch." Then he kissed her again.

Melody nestled close in his arms. "I remember every detail of every minute I ever spent with you."

He murmured into her hair, "I hope you don't mind that I proposed in front of an audience. I'll do it again if you like."

"Chad, you could ask me to marry you in front of the whole valley and the answer would still be the same."

As soon as Chad left, Melody and Lenore went to Melody's room to check her wardrobe. Her things were still strewn around the room from her earlier packing. Looking at them, Melody said, "Funny, just a few hours ago, I was planning to leave on tomorrow's stage. I never dreamed that when I left this town I would be going as Chad's bride."

Lenore smiled, "I'm so happy for you! I've been so worried about you these last two days."

"Let's see what we can find for me to wear to be married in. Oh," she said wistfully, "you should see the absolutely divine wedding dress that I have hanging at my aunt's. How I wish I had that dress here!"

"Maybe you could find something nice in Silver City."

"No, I have that new dress that we have been sewing for the church dedication next week. It will do nicely."

Lenore smiled at the idea. "With your blue bonnet that matches your eyes so prettily."

"Yes. I'll admit that I always wanted a big fancy wedding, but I think Chad is right about how he is handling things. When H. J. finds out what Chad has in mind, he is going to be furious. Anyway, I love Chad so much it doesn't matter how we get married, just as long as I belong to him forever."

The women hugged and Lenore left Melody alone. As she undressed for bed, she said, "Thank you, Lord, for not letting me kill H. J." Then she knelt by the side of her bed and prayed, "And thank you for Chad. Thank you that I didn't lose him. I know that I probably don't deserve him after what I've done, but I'll work hard to make him happy. Please bless our marriage and let us live without any more violence. Please bless what Chad is trying to do."

She lay awake for a long time wondering if her mother could see what she was doing, what would she say. "Oh, mother," she said aloud, "I really tried, but I can't do anything to make up for your losses. I loved you. Please be happy for me."

Nineteen

Chad stood in the door of Sally's Saloon waiting for his eyes to adjust to the dim light. The noise assailed his ears, smoke made his eyes water, and the odor of cheap perfume and cheap whiskey filled his nose. As he pushed his way to the bar, a hush fell across the crowded room. By now, everyone in the saloon knew that he had killed Frank Smith. Some were saying good riddance; others were saying he should have let Frank kill Farris. As he moved through the crowd, several men who were friends of Sam's slapped him on the back, and a couple offered to buy him a drink. He declined the offers, and turning to the bartender asked, "Hey, Max, is Sally busy? I need to talk to her."

Max inclined his head toward the back office; Chad went over and knocked on the door. Sally opened the door, obviously annoyed at being disturbed. When she saw who it was, she looked around nervously and pulled Chad in, closing the door behind him. "I didn't expect t' see you 'round here. I was just decidin' what I should tell yore ol' man about Frank's death. Maybe you can help me out. Word has it that you had something t' do with it."

Chad said, "I guess you could say that. Did you know that H. J. hired Frank to kill Sam?"

Her undisguised look of surprise convinced him, better than any words, that she hadn't known. Sally never had been a good liar. Quickly trying to cover up, she said, "All I know is H. J. asked me t' keep Frank posted on what was happenin' 'round town. He has been hangin' 'round here ever since he left yore place. I don't know nothin' 'bout no murder."

"But you do know that H. J. was here tonight."

The woman didn't know how to answer; Chad saved her the trouble. "Never mind, I saw him myself. All I want from you is to have Max ride out to the ranch with a message for my father."

"Why Max?"

"Because he is probably the only person who could get on the place without any trouble. Slade and all the other men know Max."

Sally opened the door and motioned to Max, who had been watching the door ever since Chad had gone in. Max came in and closed the door. Sally said to him, "He wants you to take a message to H. J."

Chad studied the man for a minute, remembering what he had heard his father say about Max. Figuring he could be trusted to deliver it right and keep his mouth shut, Chad said, "I want you to tell him that Frank is dead. I'll be in Silver City for a few days, and I'll explain everything when I get back. Got that?"

"What am I supposed t' say if he asks how Frank died?"

"I really don't care," Chad answered wearily. The day had been long and hard on him.

Sally asked, "Can it wait 'til we close up?"

"Just as long as he gets the message before morning." Chad started to go back into the saloon, changed his mind and headed for the back door.

He stepped cautiously out into the night. He got Beau, who was still tied down the street, and took him to the livery stable where he arranged with the hostler to keep him until Saturday. Renting a room in the hotel, he went right to bed, but he spent a long time going over what he had done. Killing Frank didn't set easy with him, although he knew that he would do it again in the same circumstances. Among other things, he had set up a meeting for tomorrow morning, and he wasn't entirely sure what he would say to the men.

The next morning, he was able to get Mr. Tremble to open the general store early to allow him to buy some new range clothes to replace the bloodstained things he was wearing. The store didn't have a big selection, but at least he was clean and neat. After a visit to the barber shop, he walked jauntily toward the Farrises' house. Whereas last night, he had only a vague idea of what he planned to do next, this morning he had things pretty well figured out. He wished he had Marty with him, but it was better that Marty not be in on any of this. That way, H. J. couldn't hold it against him.

When he reached the house, Lenore and Melody had breakfast all ready. Melody took a lot of teasing about her cooking and how Chad was going to like it. He smiled with pride at how beautiful she was when she blushed, and thought how lucky he was to be getting her for his bride.

After breakfast, Chad and Sam split up and, with the help of a few others, alerted as many men as possible of the meeting at eleven. The night before, Sam had sent the

Oleson boy out to tell some of the ranchers; in turn, they notified more men than Chad had hoped they could. By ten-thirty, men were already walking or riding toward the schoolhouse.

Max, on his way back from the Winslow spread, snickered a little as he saw the men heading south of town. Respectable people, he thought to himself, they are always having a fool meeting about something or other. Since he couldn't be bothered much with anything that happened before four in the afternoon, he only wondered momentarily what this one was about. Tired from being up all night, he didn't even bother to tell Sally about it. He hadn't been very happy about having to make that long ride after working all evening, especially since he expected H. J. to be livid at the news. He had felt himself very lucky that H. J. wasn't up yet. So he had given the message to Marty and left.

As the schoolhouse filled up, Chad became a little nervous. Although Sam had agreed that his idea was a good one, he didn't know how these men would feel about it. Everything depended on their agreement. Glad that he had taken the time to get to know some of them during the last weeks, he was counting on that to make them more receptive to what he had to say.

The men were of many different ages and backgrounds; some were men with prospering businesses, some small shopowners, some cattlemen with different sized spreads, some homesteaders with little except their dreams of a better life. All they had in common was a desire to live in this valley unhampered by Winslow. They grew quiet when Sam stood up and started to speak. "By now, you have all probably heard about what happened last night. What you might not know is that H. J. Winslow hired that man to kill me, figuring that it would look like a grudge match because of our earlier fight."

When he mentioned Winslow, several pairs of eyes studied Chad. Some were openly suspicious. Noticing the looks, Sam said, "I want you all to know that I wouldn't be here today if Chad Winslow hadn't stepped in and saved me. He's also the one who told me about H. J.'s part in the shooting."

"I don't trust him. I don't trust no Winslow," called out a large man near the back. Several voices muttered in agreement.

Sam looked steadily at the speaker. "You trust me, don't you?" After everyone agreed that they did, Sam went on. "Well, trust me when I tell you that Chad Winslow is a friend of mine, and I would trust him with my life. Many of you know that he is a lawyer. He has some ideas to help us straighten out our town and valley, and I want you to listen to him."

Chad got up knowing that he had to win these men over. He had the uneasy feeling that he would have to spend a lot of his life living down his father's name. He looked right at the men and said, "First off, I want you to know that I am genuinely sorry for the trouble that my father has caused many of you. I have been away at school for a long time, so I don't know everything that has happened in this valley. Much of what I do know, I am ashamed of. I love this valley as much as you do, and I want to see it grow but remain a good place to raise a family. I can't undo anything that has happened thus far, but I believe that by working together we can control what happens around here from now on."

By now, he had everyone's attention. "The key word there is together. I wonder if you ever stopped to think that all of you together represent more power than H. J. and all his hands have. If you were determined to help each other, no one would find himself in the position of having to sell to H. J."

The man in the back stood up and shouted, "It's easy for you to say. You have yore ol' man's land and money t' fall back on. What do I have if I go broke? If I don't get some water soon, I have no choice but to sell." There were several men who expressed similar opinions.

"If you let me finish, I think you will see that you do have a choice," Chad said evenly. "Also, you're wrong about my not having anything to lose. The fact that I am even talking to you means that I will lose everything my father could give me. I'll be leaving this valley in a few days, but you have to stay here and make your places work. This is all for your benefit."

The men quieted down, and Chad went on to outline several ways that they could help themselves, ending by saying, "Sam and I are going to Silver City this afternoon. If you are in agreement, we will bring a U. S. marshall back to keep an eye on things until the town is organized."

When Chad sat down, Sam got up and asked the men if they were in agreement with what had been said. After some discussion, everyone agreed; some with reservations, but most with enthusiasm, realizing for the first time that many of their problems had been caused by their divisiveness.

As soon as Chad and Sam could get away from the other men, they headed home for a quick dinner before taking the afternoon stage.

Arriving in Silver City, they went directly to the sheriff's office. Brady looked surprised to see Chad, but when he saw Sam, his face lit up. "Sam, you old son-of-a-gun, what happened to your arm? And what are you doing with the Winslow kid?"

Chad bristled a little at his last question, but Sam laughed and shook Brady's hand. "He isn't a kid, Brady. If it weren't for him, I would be dead. Shorty Johnson's friend, Frank Smith, tried to gun me down. Chad shot him."

Brady shook his head and said, "Well, Winslow, it looks like trouble seems to follow you around, but somehow you always come out all right. I'll tell you this, Sam is a good man, an' if you saved his life, then you just paid me back for savin' yours." He motioned the men to sit down and went on, "Now, what are you two doin' here?"

After Chad explained what was going on in Marysville, Brady laughed a deep, pleasant laugh. "You're really something. It takes a big man to see an' admit the faults in his own family. I guess I should have trusted my first instincts when I met you, but when you said you were a Winslow—well, I just let that fact cloud my judgement. Anyway, you aren't goin' to believe this, but I was comin' to Marysville tomorrow, myself. I was just made a deputy U. S. Marshall, partly so I would have authority in Basin River Valley. There have been so many complaints about no law there. Also, Frank Smith was wanted for murder. I assume from what you just told me that he is dead; so I can forget about him."

Chad and Sam looked at each other. Without saying a word, they both knew that Brady was exactly what Marysville needed.

Brady added, "Since I would love to be around when H. J. finds out his day is over, I think I'll just ride on over to Marysville with you two. Scott can take care of things around here. Since Shorty's hangin' things have quieted down a great deal in town. How long you figure you'll need me?"

"About two weeks or so," Sam answered.

Brady's deputy came in the door and nodded at the men. Getting up, Brady said, "Have you two eaten yet? Now that Scott's back, we can go get some supper."

After the three were seated in the dining room of the hotel, Brady asked Chad, "You plannin' on stayin' on in Basin River Valley?"

"No, I don't think I can. When I was in the capital seeing Shorty, I talked with the judge about the city's needing a lawyer to prosecute criminals. I wasn't interested then, but now I think I would like that. Remember we talked about how we would like to see law and order in this territory? I would like to be part of that—using my knowledge of the law instead of a gun to bring it about."

"Yeah, I remember our talking, but I didn't think you would ever do it. I figured you would stay on the ranch."

Chad frowned as he said, "I don't think I'll be welcome around the ranch after my marriage, and I know that Melody could never be comfortable there."

Sam laughed at the surprised look on Brady's face. "We didn't tell you about that part of his plans, did we?"

While they ate Chad told Brady all about Melody and her family, even the things she tried to do to H. J. "I guess she never did get much revenge, but she got me."

After that, they talked about the wedding plans, and Sam and Brady caught up on what had happened to each of them since they had last seen each other. Finally Chad got up, saying, "If I'm going to get that train to the capital in the morning I had better get some shut-eye. While I'm gone, I want Sam to have a doctor look at his arm. We should be ready to leave Saturday morning. You taking the stage, Brady, or were you going to ride your horse?"

"I prefer to have my own horse. I'll be in Marysville sometime Saturday afternoon. By the way, is it true that Matt Slade is workin' for H. J.?"

"Yes, do you know Slade?"

"Well, we've had a couple of brushes in the past. It should be interestin' t' see him again."

Twenty

On Saturday morning, when the stage carrying Sam and Chad arrived in Marysville, a radiant Melody and Lenore met it. As soon as the two couples had greeted each other, Melody said, "You'll never believe what's happening. We have to go to the church right now."

"What for?" Chad asked as he and Sam were pushed toward the site.

"All the men have been working on the church ever since you left Thursday, each doing as much as he could between his own chores. They decided that since it was almost finished they could have it done in time for us to be married in, if they worked all day today. Isn't that wonderful?" Melody was practically dancing with excitement.

Lenore, who was almost as pleased as Melody, said, "They said that the two of you have done so much to help the town that they wanted you to be the first ones to be married in the new church. The Reverend arrived this morning, so everything is going perfectly!"

"The women have brought enough food for everyone to stay all day, and since we will be leaving right after the service tomorrow, they want to have a little party for us today. That is all right isn't it?" She was so obviously excited about the whole thing that Chad had to go along with it, although he had hoped to have a quick, quiet service and no party.

Chad helped the men, while the women fussed over the food and chattered about the wedding. Many of these people seldom got to socialize, and they were enjoying the chance to get together. They all enjoyed a great deal of fun at Melody and Chad's expense. Shortly before dinner, Marshall Brady came riding up.

"As I rode by I noticed all this activity and figured you would be here," he said to Sam, who had come to greet him. The men all quit working and gathered around Brady while Sam introduced him.

After dinner, Chad drew Sam aside and said, "I have to go out to the ranch for a while, but I don't want Melody to come along. It could get nasty."

Sam nodded his understanding and asked, "You want Brady or me to come with you?"

"No, I'll be all right. I don't think anyone out there is ready to shoot at me—yet," he answered with a frown. "If I'm not back before dark, you might send Brady to look for me."

"Did you tell Melody that you're going?"

"Yes. She isn't too happy about it, but it has to be done. Would you see that she gets her things to the stage office? Have them sent to the capital. That way we'll have to bother only with a few personal things. We will be leaving after the wedding to spend the night in Silver City. We'll probably go on to the capital the next day. I'll feel a lot better getting Melody away from here."

"I'll be glad to help," Sam said, shaking Chad's hand. "You be careful."

Chad caught Melody's eye and nodded to her before

he left the room. He walked to the livery stable and got Beau. Telling the hostler that they would be taking the horses away the next afternoon, he paid the bill for Beau and Fortune.

He didn't much enjoy the ride to the ranch, figuring it could be the last time he would make it. Things seemed quiet enough as he rode into the yard. He was pleased to find Marty in the corral since he wanted to talk to him alone before confronting his father. Walking over to Marty, Chad punched him on the arm as he had for years. Marty looked him over as if inspecting a new horse. "Where you been? H. J. has been hollerin' fer ya since Max delivered yore message. What was that bit about Frank? I figured he'd left these parts by now."

"Believe it or not, H. J. never really fired Frank. Seems he had Frank in town to keep an eye on Sam Farris. Then he paid Frank to kill Sam."

Marty swore under his breath. "Chad, are you sure?"

"Yeah, Marty. I'm sure. I myself saw the money exchange hands. I had to shoot him, but I didn't like the feeling much. From now on, I hope to do my fighting in court—not with a gun."

Marty nodded in understanding before saying, "The ol' man ain't gonna be none too happy 'bout you killin' Frank 'fore he got the job done."

"The ol' man isn't going to be very happy about anything I've done since I left here." Chad put his arm around his friend's shoulder as they started walking toward the house. "I'm going to marry Melody Chaffin tomorrow morning."

"Melody Chaffin! You mean. . . "

"That's right. She is the little girl that was at the Chaffin's house when you took her father home. Marty, I think she is beginning to come around to accepting that you shot her father to save your friend. Someday, I hope she can forget the whole incident. I want you to know that we will be living in the capital. If you ever need me for anything, don't hesitate to come to me for help."

"You won't be 'round here? I don't understand."

"You will when we get through in here," Chad said, opening the front door.

They found H. J. in his office talking with Slade. Chad said, "Slade, I want to talk to my father alone."

Slade eased himself out of the chair he was sprawled in. His glance moved to Marty, standing in the doorway. He said, "If ya want t' talk t' him alone, what's he doin' here?"

"Marty belongs here; you don't," Chad answered.

Slade started to say something, but H. J. nodded toward the door. Slade walked out. Marty stepped aside while he passed, evenly meeting Slade's glance. Marty closed the door and sat in the nearest chair, wondering what was going on.

H. J. shouted at Chad, "Where in tarnation you been? And what was that message supposed to mean?"

Chad walked calmly over to his father's desk, pulled the gun and the handkerchief with the bloodstained money out of his coat, and threw them in front of him. The money spilled out as he said, "I believe these belong to you. You see, Frank didn't earn the money. I shot him first."

H. J. started to protest, but Chad said evenly, "Don't bother denying it. I saw you give him the money and the gun."

"If you knew I wanted Farris dead, why the hell did you interfere?"

"For one thing, Sam Farris is a good friend of mine, and I wouldn't stand by and see anyone shoot him. Besides, that's not the way to deal with a problem. You can't go on doing away with everyone who crosses you. Before you start cussing and shouting at me, I might as well tell you that I don't intend to put up with it. I have several things to say to you, and I would suggest for your own good that you listen to what I've got to say." Chad stood in front of the desk, looking down at his father as he talked.

Startled at his son's aggressive manner, H. J. sat quietly while Chad continued. "First off, I'm going to be married in town tomorrow morning, but you're not invited. The reason is that her name is Melody Chaffin, and she holds you responsible for the deaths of her brother and father. Second, Sheriff Brady from Silver City is now a deputy U. S. marshall, and he will be in Marysville for the next few weeks. He will be keeping a close watch on you; so I would suggest you keep your nose clean. Specifically, if anything were to happen to Sam Farris, you would be the one Brady would come for."

H. J. smirked at the last remark, saying, "He can't stay 'round here forever."

"You're right. However, there will be an election in the next couple of weeks to elect a mayor, counsel, and sheriff for Marysville. Brady will be here long enough to get the new sheriff settled in his job." Chad paused to let the news sink in. Then he went on, "The local people have also formed a loose association with the intention of standing together. You'll never buy out anyone dirt cheap again. No more cattlemen versus homesteaders— from now on it is going to be everybody versus Winslow. Oh, yes, and one thing that is going to help them is the matter of your dam. You probably already know this, but I carefully checked, and the land you have the dam on is mine. Mother left it to me. The borders of your land are well below the river fork. As far as I'm concerned, you can still use any of my land for grazing, but I want that dam off my property. Brady will be out to check on it in a few days. If it is still there, he has my orders to have it blown up. From now on, everyone in this valley has an equal chance at the water."

Chad looked sadly at his father, who was starting to look a little confused. "I want you to know that I haven't forgotten the man you used to be to me or the education you gave me. In one way, I still care about you, and I'm doing this as much for you as for the others."

"You call ruinin' me doin' somethin' for me?"

"If you keep on the way you're going, you will either end up shot from ambush or hanged for shooting someone. I don't want to see you die like that. You have enough land and water to keep you going strong. The only difference is that now you'll not be able to rule over this valley."

H. J. spoke with pleading in his voice, "But, son, don't you know that I just wanted t' keep the valley the way it was so you an' yore sons could have it? I did it for you as much as myself."

"Sorry, H. J., I don't buy that. You wanted your name to go on forever in this valley, and that's a lot different than caring about me personally. I have one last piece of news. Since you are the reason there is no one to carry on the Chaffin name, I plan on naming my first son Mark Chaffin. I even thought about changing my name, but I've decided to try and make Winslow a name a man can be proud of again."

Seeing that he wasn't getting anywhere with Chad, H. J. reverted back to anger. "It's that girl! You stupid fool! Don't you realize that she is just usin' you t' get back at me for somethin' she imagines I did?"

"You're wrong, H. J. She doesn't even realize what's happening. She came back here to get revenge on you. In fact, she was the one who cut the fences, burned the barn, and tried to blow up the dam, but she eventually gave up. It's ironic, isn't it, that when she fell in love with me and gave up her idea to get even with you, she got the best kind of revenge—you took the Chaffin son and now you are going to lose your son and heir. Melody doesn't even know that I want to name my son after her brother, so you can't blame her for that."

"What do you plan t' live on? That little bit of land you own wouldn't do you much good. You need me just t' make it," H. J. said with a ring of triumph to his voice.

"I don't want anything of yours. I want you to understand that. This place is yours and it should be half Marty's—as I've said many times. The money I inherited from Mother's family is in the bank at Silver City, and I can manage on that until I make some more. I will be working in the capital for a while." Chad started for the door. "I will take Beau, the buggy I bought to court Melody, and my books and some personal things. Other than that I don't want anything from you—ever. Everything you have is stained with blood."

Marty, who had been totally silent during the whole conversation, quietly got up and followed Chad out the door. H. J. shouted after them, "You'll be back. Just you wait and see. Someday, you'll want something from me, an' then my money won't seem so dirty t' you."

While Chad was getting his things together and saying goodbye to a tearful Rosie, Marty hitched Beau up to Chad's buggy. The horse had pulled the buggy before, but he didn't like it much. Marty was ill at ease about the turn of events. He knew that H. J. wouldn't give up that easily, and the knowledge weighed heavily on him. Even though he had always backed up H. J., he felt Chad was doing the right thing. A man has to be proud of his father and of his family name if he wants to live in peace with himself.

When the young man had finished loading his things in the buggy, he gave Marty an impulsive and self-conscious hug, and said, "Marty, why don't you come with me? I hate to leave you with this mess. H. J. is going to make life pretty miserable for everyone around here—especially you."

Marty glanced toward the house, where he knew H. J. was conferring with Slade. "No, Chad, I have a job to do right here. Take care of yourself, son." He wanted to say much more, but the two men understood each other well enough that a lot of words weren't necessary. Chad spoke to Beau and started for Marysville.

Marty busied himself around the barn, as if waiting for something. As he waited, he took out his Colt .45, slipped a cartridge in the empty chamber under the hammer, spun the cylinder around, and dropped the gun lightly into his holster. From a long ago habit, he tied the holster to his leg. As he did, he remembered telling Chad that he would never kill again except for someone he loved. "This is for you, Chad," he said to the fast disappearing figure.

Inside the house, H. J. was ranting at Slade about Chad's betrayal. "It's all that blasted Chaffin woman's fault. If she wasn't around fillin' his head with lies, he would see reason. Do you have any qualms about killin' women?" he asked the gunfighter, who was draped across the biggest chair in the room.

An ugly sneer contorted Slade's mouth. "They die jest like a man does."

"Good. I want you t' go int' town an' get rid of that woman. Since you're ridin' alone, you can probably get there before Chad does in the buggy. Do you remember what she looks like? We saw her with Chad one day on the road."

"A man don't forget a woman what looks like that one."
He uncurled himself from the chair. "It won't be any problem. You want the kid dead, too?"

"No! I want him back here. That boy has my blood and my name. Remember that idiot marshall is in town."

"I've run int' Brady before. He don't worry me none."

After Slade left the room, H. J. sat and stared at a painting of Mary and Chad that hung on his wall. "I always had such big dreams for you," he said to the picture.

Outside, Marty watched Slade saddle his horse, and then walked around so he was about twenty feet behind him. He knew what could happen at that close range, and he was counting on it. In a calm voice, he asked, "Goin' somewhere, Slade?"

Slade didn't even turn around as he answered, "If it's any of yore business, I have somethin' t' do fer the boss. Somethin' he knows you're not man enough t' do."

Marty put his hand on his gun and said in a low, even voice that held a challenge, "No, Slade. I don't think you'll be doin' anythin' fer him, ever again."

Slade turned then and faced Marty, pushing his coat back and stroking his gun. His eyes blazed with anger and his upper lip curled in a sneer. "Ya plannin' on stoppin' me? I've been wonderin' when ya would try t' take me. I've heard it said that ya used t' be pretty fast."

Two hands flashed; two guns cracked. A look of anguished surprise crossed Slade's ugly face as he realized that Marty was as fast as he was.

Hearing the shots, H. J. came running out of the house to find the two men lying in their own blood. As H. J. Winslow knelt beside the only real friend he ever had, Chad was riding toward Marysville and Melody—the nester's daughter.